Discover for yourself why readers can't get enough of the multiple award-winning publisher Ellora's Cave. Whether you prefer e-books or paperbacks, be sure to visit EC on the web at www.ellorascave.com for an erotic reading experience that will leave you breathless.

www.ellorascave.com

Ellora's Cave Publishing, Inc.
PO Box 787
Hudson, OH 44236-0787

ISBN # 184360647X

THINGS THAT GO BUMP IN THE NIGHT, 2003.
ALL RIGHTS RESERVED
Ellora's Cave Publishing, Inc.
© NAUGHTY NANCY, JAID BLACK, 2001.
© BLOODLUST, MARILYN LEE, 2001.
© A LITTLE TOO CHARMING, TREVA HARTE, 2001.

This book may not be reproduced in whole or in part without author and publisher permission.

Edited by Cris Brashear and Tina Engler.
Cover art by Tina Engler.

Warning: The following material contains strong sexual content meant for mature readers. THINGS THAT GO BUMP IN THE NIGHT has been rated NC17 erotic, by a minimum of three independent reviewers. We strongly suggest storing this book in a place where young readers not meant to view it are unlikely to happen upon it. That said, enjoy…

THINGS THAT GO BUMP IN THE NIGHT

Naughty Nancy – Part I
By Jaid Black
-5-

Bloodlust
By Marilyn Lee
-15-

A Little To Charming
By Treva Harte
-87-

Naughty Nancy – Part II
By Jaid Black
-131-

Naughty Nancy –
Book 4 ½: Trek Mi Q'an
Part I

By Jaid Black

Prologue

Nancy Lombardo bit down onto her bottom lip as her eyes shifted warily toward the old woman. She had to be a witch, she thought. In a town like Salem, Massachusetts—and on Halloween night no less!—she couldn't be anything but a witch.

Either that or an extremely eccentric looking homeless person with a penchant for wearing black robes and loud blue eyeshadow while she stood there stirring only God knows what around in a cauldron as she chanted in what sounded to be Latin.

Nancy sighed. She really should have taken that job in Anchorage. The weirdest thing she would have had to worry about encountering in Alaska was getting kidnapped by a lonely mountain man who hadn't laid eyes on a woman since his inbred wife had passed on to—wherever it is inbred wives pass on to.

Nancy's back went ramrod straight as she continued walking down the dark alley. She refused to be afraid, she sniffed. This was her night, damn it. The night she was going to saunter into her friend Lori's party and shine like the belle of the ball.

No more wallflower Nancy. No more being the fat girl out. No more watching through the spectacles perched on the end of her nose as men looked past her to the dimwitted idiots standing behind her with the buffed bodies and the unbuffed brains. Tonight *she* was going to be one of those dimwitted idiots with the buffed bodies and the unbuffed brains, she thought with a harrumph.

Well okay, so she wasn't exactly dimwitted. And her body wasn't exactly buffed. And, she grimly conceded, she had graduated at the top of her class in law school.

Her lips pinched together in a frown. *Damn it!*

"'Tis naught tae worry aboot," the old woman croaked out, causing Nancy to lose her train of thought.

"Huh?" Nancy's gaze shot toward where the old woman had been stirring her cauldron—the very same black-clad figure who had been standing on the opposite side of the alley, but who had somehow managed to land directly in front of her. "Goodness," she breathed out as her hand instinctively flew up to shield her heart, "you scared me."

The old woman's weathered face crinkled into what on most people would be considered a smile. On her it looked more like a pasty slit in between a bunch of equally pasty wrinkles.

Nancy swallowed a bit nervously as she waited to see what the old woman wanted. She absently adjusted her Xena the warrior princess costume and shifted the sword belt to the side. She winced and moved it back. The tip of the sword kept poking through its scabbard and jabbing her in the thigh.

Damn it!

"Can I help you with something?" Nancy asked in clipped tones, her voice unnaturally harsh. Call her a tad on the defensive side but it was Halloween night and the old woman gave her the creeps. She kept staring into her eyes as if searching for something, but otherwise the mysterious witch remained silent.

A suspended moment passed in eerie quiet as the two women locked eyes. It gave Nancy enough time to let the guilt settle in. She sighed. "I didn't mean to yell at you," she said quietly, her expression apologetic. She smiled. "I guess we all get a little freaked out on a night like this." She decided to ignore the fact that the old woman was the reason she was freaked out to begin with.

"'Twill be a long journey," the old witch murmured. Her palm came up and rested on Nancy's forehead as she continued to study her face. "But 'twill be worth the sacrifices when all is said and done. And love shall be yers."

Nancy's eyes darted back and forth as the old woman began to chant. She nibbled on her bottom lip.

Back in law school Nancy had been taught how to effectively deal with many different types of bizarre situations, but this one had definitely not been covered in any of the college texts. When the old woman's chanting picked up to a fevered squeal akin to the sound a pig might make when being slaughtered for Sunday dinner, she felt her cheeks redden.

Nope, definitely not covered in the law school texts.

Damn it!

"Are you okay?" Nancy asked wearily. She tried to politely remove the old crone's palm from her forehead, but the wrinkled thing wouldn't budge. She absently wondered if the old woman had been an arm wrestler in her heyday. "Do you need an aspirin or something?" Her tongue darted out to wet her lips as the squealing grew shriller. "I think I have a stick of gum tucked away in my scabbard if you—"

Nancy blinked. Her breath caught in the back of her throat.

The old woman was gone.

"Good grief," she mumbled as her head darted back and forth. "Where did she go?"

After a suspended moment of just standing there with her mouth agape—no doubt looking like the village idiot—she shook her head and sighed. She really should have taken that job in Anchorage.

Straightening her back regally, Nancy dismissed the oddity of the situation from her mind and continued to walk down the dark alley. She could hear music and laughter floating out of a window a ways down, which could only mean she was almost at the old warehouse Lori had renovated for tonight's Halloween party.

Nancy took a deep breath as she wondered for the fiftieth time since she'd left her apartment an hour ago what everyone would think of her new look. Not the Xena costume itself, but the bodily changes that had gone along with it. During her two-month leave of absence from the law firm, she had used the time to completely transform her image.

Gone was the schoolmarm bun she had always tightly wrapped her hair into, and in its place was a sultry mane of light brown cascading hair, which her stylist had thoughtfully added golden highlights to. Gone was the spinsterish pair of oversized spectacles that had always sat suspended on the tip of her nose, and in its place were a pair of translucent contact lenses that showed off the rich chocolate brown of her eyes.

And, she thought with much relief, gone were those extra forty pounds of bulk. In their place was a voluptuous form that was beginning to show the first signs of muscle tone from daily exercise and sensible eating. She wasn't skinny and knew she never would be, in fact she was still somewhat fleshy, but for the first time in years she looked and felt healthy.

The Xena outfit was more than a costume to her, she realized. It was the very symbolism of the new Nancy Lombardo, a Nancy Lombardo who was no longer content to sit on the sidelines as a passive spectator while life passed her by. She was an alpha female now. A warrior woman. A warrior woman who hadn't had sex since three presidents ago.

Damn it!

But that pitiful circumstance would change tonight, she reassured herself as she straightened her shoulders and walked determinedly up the back steps that would take her to the renovated warehouse loft above. Times were changing. The wallflower had died. She was a phoenix rising up from the flames of abject grief and despair. She was—

Bah! Times were changing. Enough said.

Nancy took a calming breath as she pushed open the warehouse doors and strolled inside. She instantly forgot about her nervousness as she glanced around, the smile on her face indicative of her festive mood. The old Stapleton warehouse looked great.

Lori had decorated the place perfectly, the dark atmosphere and lit jack-o-lanterns scattered about setting just the right mood. Skeletons stood across the room at either side of the buffet table, grimly guarding the different sweets and appetizers that had been set out for the hungry guests. The music playing in the background had a New Age, gothic feel to it. She loved it. The old warehouse looked perfect.

"Nancy! Is that you? Wow!"

Nancy's head snapped to attention as a beautiful, vivacious redhead strolled up to her side. She smiled. Janna looked great tonight dressed in a slinky little witch's get-up that emphasized the curviness of her body. "Yep, it's me," she said as she grinned. "How's life at the ad agency treating you these days?"

Janna groaned as she rolled her eyes. "Busy. I even have to work later tonight if you can believe it."

"On Halloween? You're kidding!"

"Afraid not."

"You're not staying at Lori's party then?"

Janna embraced her in a hug, the two friends not having seen each other during Nancy's entire two month long absence. "I'll be here for another hour or so, but I have to cut out early." She sighed. "There's a man my firm is interested in hiring on and I have to go lure him into the familial fold as it were."

"How exciting," Nancy said dryly.

"Exactly." Janna grinned. "But enough of me—look at you! Nancy you look head to toe terrific."

Unused to compliments of a physical nature, Nancy found herself blushing. "Thank-you."

Janna patted her on the shoulder. "Go mingle while I use the little witch's room. I'll be right back."

Nancy chuckled. "Will do."

After Janna left her side, Nancy took her first thorough look around at the other invited guests. To her utter amazement and delight, she found more than one pair of male eyes flicking over her new form and checking her out. Flustered by the attention, and as unused to it as she was to compliments, she nervously lifted her hand to push the spectacles up the bridge of her nose only to realize halfway there that she wasn't wearing any.

Damn it!

She took a deep breath. She could do this. She could mingle with the male guests and behave as natural in a social setting as any other woman would. She was more than a woman, she reminded herself. She was a warrior woman. Xena. Phoenix from the—

Bah! She could do this. Enough said.

Her chin going up a notch, Nancy firmly told herself that she would—right now at this very moment in time—join the party and seek out an attractive male to talk to. A simple thing to most women, perhaps, but a portent symbolism to herself.

Strolling further into the renovated warehouse loft, the next person Nancy's gaze clashed with was not a male's, however, but another one of her closest female friends. She grinned at the hooker costume Erica was wearing, thinking she looked absolutely gorgeous in it. But then again, Erica looked gorgeous in anything she wore with her statuesque, blonde good looks.

Erica's eyes lit up as her gaze flicked up and down Nancy's body. Nancy couldn't be certain from across the room, but she could have sworn she'd seen Erica mouth the word "wow". Nancy was about to approach her friend for a hug when a tall man dressed like Count Dracula appeared seemingly out of nowhere and stalked determinedly up to Erica's side.

Nancy blinked. Old women magically disappearing. Tall, handsome men magically appearing. What a night.

Deciding she would wait and talk to Erica later, she smiled and waved at her friend rather than intrude on the conversation that Dracula was attempting to engage her in. Besides, she reminded herself, it was time to quit stalling and find a man to chat with. Erica would be pleased with her decision. She was always trying to set Nancy up on blind dates with various, assorted men of her acquaintance.

Taking what felt like her millionth calming breath of the evening, Nancy adjusted her sword belt and resumed her stroll through the throng of guests. Tonight, she would get a life. Tonight, she would find a man. Tonight, she would end the bitter solitude of not having known a man's bed since big hair had been in fashion. Tonight, she would—

Bah! She would get some cock tonight if it killed her. Enough said.

Bloodlust

By Marilyn Lee

Chapter One

Erica Kalai resisted the urge to tug at her short, tight, form-hugging dress in an effort to get it to cover more of her body. It was useless. The black dress she wore ended so far above her knees that nearly all her stocking clad thighs were exposed. There just wasn't enough material to pull down and the dress was cut so low that any one with half an eye would have an excellent view of her breasts.

Now, at the party, was a fine time to decide that coming as a hooker might not have been such a good idea. She *was* dressed as a hooker and she *was* there. She might as well make the best of it. She would make the best of it. It wasn't every day a woman turned 40 and she meant to enjoy her night out.

Still, she hated to think what the teenage girls she taught at an exclusive private school just outside Boston would say if they could see their "respectable" instructor stalking around a renovated loft in spiked heels, blatantly looking as if she were on the prowl for cock. She thought about the condoms tucked in the tiny leather bag hanging off her shoulder and was thankful for the overall dark atmosphere of the interior. Her cheeks burned. She *was* on the prowl for cock.

After the breakup of her five-year marriage, she had spent so much time trying to fix up her friend Nancy that her own love life had suffered—a deliberate refusal to deal with her wariness, she knew, for she hadn't been all that eager to get out and start meeting men again. In fact, if not for her and Nancy's mutual friend Janna, she probably wouldn't even have come tonight.

She glanced around, taking a sip of the spiked apple cider. From what she could see all the men here appeared to be at least ten years her junior. She thought of the old woman she'd encountered in the alley as she arrived and tossed her head disdainfully. *Love would be hers indeed.* Forget love. After two years without a significant other, she would happily settle for a one-night stand with a man with a nice, stiff dick. It wouldn't even need to be large or thick—just hard. But unless she planned to rob the cradle, she wouldn't likely see any action tonight.

Not that she had much about which to complain. At least she didn't have to spend part of her Halloween night working like poor Janna. Because of the excessive hours Janna had been putting in lately, all their recent contact had been by phone.

She glanced around. Instead of spotting her pretty red-haired friend, her eyes locked with those of a man across the length of the warehouse. Her breath caught in her throat and she found she couldn't look away. He was tall, dark, and handsome with a capital H.

Who was he? Where had he come from? He hadn't stood next to the jack-o-lanterns just minutes before…

No way she wouldn't have noticed him. Not only was he dressed as her favorite anti-hero, Count Dracula, but more to the point, he stood there staring first at her exposed breasts and then into her eyes. While she was used to men staring, she'd never looked into a pair of eyes as dark or as compelling as this man's. Nor had she ever seen a man who oozed sex appeal from every pore in his body. Even sharing his gaze from across the room caused a stirring between her legs.

Abruptly, the man casually tossed back the cape he wore and cast a quick look down. Her gaze followed his and she sucked in a breath, her heart suddenly thumping in her chest. There, against the side of his leg, she saw the clear outline of a long, thick cock.

She stared at it, slowly and unthinkingly licking her lips, her cunt beginning to pulse with unbridled hunger. A lonely, sex-starved woman could surely enjoy a long, lustful one-night stand with a man packing that kind of piece.

But what was she thinking? She, who was always warning her students against the dangers of allowing teenage boys to talk them out of their clothes and into bed? She forced her gaze back to his face. He had the most sensual lips she'd ever seen on a man, she *knew* they would be honey sweet. And those eyes—dark and magnetic. Someone had once said the eyes were the windows to the soul. She felt as if he were trying to drain the soul from her with his gaze alone. What was more, it was working—big time.

But she was being ridiculous. The spiked cider, the incessant beat of the music, along with the raw sensuality of the handsome stranger dressed as Dracula, all combined to help loosen her grip on reality. Okay, she'd fantasized about meeting a man as forceful and compelling as The Count since she'd first read Dracula. However, she was no longer an impressible fifteen-year-old. She had no reason to stand staring at a stranger's cock—a young stranger at that. She might be horny, but...

She wrenched her gaze away, looked across the room and then did a double take as she saw Janna walking away from a woman dressed as Xena. Could that be...no. It couldn't be Nancy.

She looked again, and this time her eyes met the woman's. It was Nancy! Even as she smiled in surprised delight and uttered a small, "wow," at the new Nancy, she was aware that the stranger still stared at her from across the room.

Only he was no longer across the room. She felt a sudden tingling sensation down her neck and in her cunt and turned quickly to find him at her side. She looked up into his eyes. It must be the flickering flame from the jack-o-lanterns that caused his eyes to glow and pulse with tiny, smothering embers.

"Hello."

His voice was low and deep and danced along her nerve endings like a sweet, irresistible caress.

"Oh. Hello." Her voice came out in a breathless whisper that embarrassed her.

He smiled, revealing even white teeth, and extended his hand. "Mikhel Dumont."

"Erica Kalai." She placed her hand in his.

"It's a pleasure to meet you, Erica."

A feeling of utter delight permeated her as he locked his gaze with hers, then lifted her hand to his mouth and kissed it. Although his lips were gentle, she saw rampant lust blazing in his dark gaze. Of course she could be mistaken. She cast a quick look down at his leg.

She was not mistaken. The evidence of his arousal was still clearly visible.

She glanced up again, blushing as she met his gaze. What would he think of a woman who couldn't keep her eyes off his cock? She might be a closet wanton, but she wasn't terribly bold in real life.

Feeling flustered, she tugged her hand away from his. Instead of releasing it, he captured the other one and gently urged her toward him.

"Dance with me, Erica."

She hesitated. She didn't want to accept, but he wore an aura of power and authority as elegantly and as effortlessly as he did his costume. How, she thought on a mental sigh, could a woman resist that?

Not only did she readily allow him to draw her into his arms, but she shamelessly pressed her lower body forward until she could feel the beguiling outline of his cock. A ball of heat and desire tightened in her stomach and sent a shock of yearning careening straight down to her toes.

God she had to have him.

They moved slowly around the room, not in time to the rhythm of the music, but rather in time to a primitive tattoo that seemed to envelop and isolate them in a world all their own. A small part of her mind was still aware that many other people surrounded them. But her heart, her desire, her physical need was aware of him only.

He placed a finger under her chin and lifted her face to his. She reluctantly opened her eyes and looked up into his fiery gaze. "I want you to leave with me."

"What? I can't." Even as she spoke, she knew she as going to go with him. "I-I can't."

"Why not?"

"Why not?" There was something about him that made it difficult for her to do anything but want him. She blinked and gave her head a little shake. This was ridiculous—he'd barely spoken two sentences to her. "I...don't even know you."

He caressed her cheek with a long finger. His eyes burned with intensity. "That's all the more reason to leave with me...to get to know me," he murmured.

"You're too young," she hedged, glancing away. "You look about twenty-five."

He pressed his finger against her lips and a tingle ran through her. "Would it make you feel better if I were thirty?"

"That's still about ten years too young. Mikhel, I'm forty. Tonight."

"Tonight?" He smiled and suddenly twirled her around before spinning her back into his arms. "Happy birthday, Erica."

Laughing and feeling breathless despite herself, she looked up into his eyes. "Thank you, but that's about ten years too old to leave with you."

His eyes memorized her face. "And what if I tell you that I like older women, Erica?"

Oh, boy, but she liked the way he spoke her name, letting it roll slowly off his tongue like the last drop of vintage wine he was both eager to consume while at the same time loathed to finish.

She bit her lip. "You...you do?"

His smile was slow, full. "Yes. I do. Come with me and I'll show you how much I like older women," he said in low tones.

He bent so close to her that she felt his breath brush against her lips in a gesture that was as erotic as a kiss. She pressed closer, totally unable to resist him and the powerful sexual magnetism emanating from him. She felt—compelled.

"Come with me, Erica," he murmured.

She blinked, finding herself again, then took a deep breath. "I...I can't. I have friends here I haven't seen in weeks. I can't just leave with you."

"Why not?" His arm tightened around her waist, drawing her closer. The feel of his cock against her belly drove the last vestige of rational thought from her mind. Why not indeed? Nancy and Janna would understand. "Okay," she heard herself whisper.

"You won't be sorry," he promised in a soft, deep voice.

She believed him. She knew she was in for a long, deliciously wicked night. Later, when she was back in Boston, she would probably be ashamed of herself, horrified that it had been this easy for a man to hop into bed with her for a one-night stand.

She looked up into the dark, mesmerizing eyes of the man holding her so closely. Forget that nonsense. No way she was going to regret a moment of her time spent with this man. She nodded. "I know."

He smiled, and an absolutely delicious warmth infused her. "I'll make this a very special night for you, Erica. For us both."

She tore her gaze away from him. Across the length of the warehouse, she spotted Janna. Her friend looked bored. She couldn't see Nancy among all the people now in the loft. Feeling guilty, she waved at Janna and allowed herself to be led from the party.

Chapter Two

Keeping his gaze on the road ahead of him, Mikhel was nevertheless very aware of the woman seated beside him in the dark interior of the car, more aware than he'd ever been of any other woman. The soft scent of her perfume tickled his nose enticingly. His nostrils flared slightly—the faint, but unmistaken aroma of her arousal inflamed his senses. His cock throbbed and swelled with need. The blood pounded through his veins. The hunger for her body and her blood threatened to overwhelm him.

Eager to get her alone and into bed, he'd even begrudged the time it took to stop at her hotel for a change of clothing for the following day. Now, he guided the car into the parking lot of the waterfront restaurant where he'd decided to take her for dinner. He turned to look at her, his thirst for her blood increasing. Everything about this woman excited him—her tall voluptuous body, her big breasts, her blond hair, the soft sound of her voice, the unashamed way she looked at his cock…

Even her name fascinated him, feeding his hunger for her. He had to have her in his bed, feel her pussy accepting his cock, taste her blood on his tongue and in his mouth. His hunger increasing with every passing second, he longed to skip dinner, take her straight to bed, and as he made love to her, sink his teeth into her long, delicate neck. He would not hurt her. He couldn't hurt her. He frowned. Nor would he let anyone else hurt her.

He had spent the last twenty years searching for the one woman whose body and blood would create an insatiable need in him. The effect she had on him could only mean one thing: she was the one, his bloodlust partner. He knew of at least two full-blood females who wouldn't be happy, but this was his life and he would live it how he liked, with the bloodlust partner of his choice — Erica Kalai. His Erica Kalai.

He *would* have her. But he wanted her to come to him of her own accord, not because he'd subjugated her will with his.

Two hours later, sitting at a table overlooking the water, he fastened his gaze on her. He found her, and everything about her, intoxicating. Looking at her, talking to her — he loved it all…but he wanted more.

After several moments of silence, she put down her coffee cup and arched a brow at him. "Mikhel, you're staring — again — still."

He didn't apologize. "You're beautiful both in body and spirit. Of course I'm staring," he murmured.

Her cheeks reddened. "Okay, I can accept and appreciate that you think I'm pretty in form, but in spirit also? How can you possibly know that after one dance and one dinner?"

Watching her, an unexpected tenderness welled inside him, something he'd never felt for any woman other than his mother and sister. He smiled. "I can see the beauty of your spirit and soul in your eyes."

"It's not my eyes you've been staring at or into, it's my neck."

"That's lovely too. Long and slender, tender."

"Tender?" She laughed. "I think you're letting that costume get to you. You make me sound like a piece of meat you plan to eat for dinner!"

"Oh, make no mistake, Erica, I do plan to eat you for dinner or at least for dessert." His dark gaze flicked over her, his intentions obvious. "Your lips, your neck, your breasts, your pussy. I intend to eat and taste them all." And when he had, he intended to drink her warm blood.

He watched as a fresh surge of color stained her cheeks. She gulped. "Oh, God," she muttered unthinkingly under her breath, "you are making me so hot and horny."

Laughing, he reached out and cradled one of her hands in his. Her blush turned impossibly deeper, realizing as she now did that he had heard her thoughtlessly uttered words. "That's the plan, my Erica, to make you so hot and horny, you're as hungry for me as I am for you."

She fanned herself with a hand. "Mission accomplished, buddy."

"In that case…" He lifted her hand to his mouth and brushed his lips across the fingers. His gaze never strayed from her face. "Tell me more about yourself."

She shook her head. "I've told you everything there is to know really. I'm basically very dull. There's not much to tell beyond the fact that I'm divorced and a teacher, which you already know. I'd rather talk about you."

His standard reply to such a line was to say he was single, headed a security firm in Boston and then take the woman in question to bed. He smiled at her. "I talk much better in bed. Join me in my hotel room and I'll tell you everything you want to know."

Just for a moment he thought she would refuse, forcing him to decide between letting her exercise her free will or compelling her to accompany him. Suddenly, she averted her gaze and nodded. "All right."

He paid the check and they left the restaurant, holding hands. In the hotel elevator, he swept her into the circle of his arms and buried his face against her neck. The feel of the blood pulsing through her veins made his cock so hard it ached. He licked and kissed her neck, repeatedly fighting the impulse to bare his incisors and sink them into her lovely, warm skin.

She trembled in his arms and he felt her heart thudding against him. The thought that she might be just a little afraid of him helped cool his need to immediately taste her blood. He wanted her to freely bare her neck for him, inviting him to drink her blood.

Shuddering with a combination of pussy lust and blood lust, he pulled his mouth from her neck, tipped up her chin, and looked down into her eyes. "Do you know what I am, my Erica? Do you understand what I need from you tonight besides your beautiful body?"

Her forehead crinkled in confusion. "What do you mean do I know what you are? You're a security consultant."

He stroked her cheek. "This isn't just a costume, my Erica, as you'll soon see.

"It's not just a…" She stared up at him, her eyes widening with unmistakable fear. "Oh, God, no! Mikhel! This is a joke! It's Halloween. You're pulling my leg."

He bared his teeth, allowing her to see his sharpened incisors. "It's not a joke. I'm just what you think I am, my Erica."

She stumbled back against the elevator wall. "Oh, God! You're frightening me. There are no much things as…as…"

"Vampires?" He closed the distance between them and touched her cheek. She gasped and recoiled, but there was nowhere for her to go, her back was already at the wall. "There are such things, my Erica, but you have no need to fear me. I will never hurt you. Never, my Erica."

She gulped in several deep breaths. "Okay. This is getting way too weird. Please. Let me go, Mikhel."

The elevator door opened behind them and he spun around. A man and a woman stood there, both dressed as vampires. He bared his incisors and growled low in his throat, "Take the next one!"

The couple gasped and stumbled back from the elevator and he pushed the button to close the door. When he turned back to face Erica, her face had lost nearly all its color, her eyes were wide and unblinking. He could hear her heart thumping in fear.

He sighed, retracted his incisors, and stretched out a hand. Although she cringed, she allowed him to take her hand in his. "Don't be afraid, my Erica. Please." He drew her trembling body in his arms and held her tightly, rocking her. "I will never hurt you. Never." He cupped her face in his hands and stared down into her eyes. "I won't do anything to you that you don't want me to do. I promise. Trust me, my Erica."

Trust a man she'd never met before who was telling her he was a vampire? "Oh, Mikhel!" She buried her face against his shoulder. "Part of me wants you, but another part of me is afraid."

"Trust the part that wants me, my Erica and never, never fear me. I won't hurt you or let anyone else hurt you. Will you willingly come with me? If you really want, I'll take you back to the party, but I really need you to stay with me tonight. Will you?"

She lifted her face and looked up at him.

He forced himself not to coerce her in any way.

His heart thumped in his chest and he experienced an incredible sense of joy when she nodded.

"Yes. I'll stay," whispered.

* * * * *

Standing with Mikhel in the moonlight in front of the big floor to ceiling windows in his hotel room, Erica had never been more afraid in her life. And yet, she'd never felt more alive, more sensual, more lustful.

Looking up into his dark, glowing eyes, she knew that he was in fact a vampire, that he intended to drink her blood. Nevertheless, the tenderness of his mouth as he kissed her lips and the gentleness of his hands as he carefully removed her shoes, her short, tight dress, her panty hose, and finally her lace underwear lessened her fears.

Maybe she was foolish to believe herself safe with him, but she couldn't quite believe he meant to hurt her. When she was naked, she stood with her heart beating wildly, her mouth dry as he slowly moved around her, frankly assessing her body.

She bit her lip. Although she'd managed to keep her weight under control, her body wasn't as firm or as supple as it used to be. Okay, so her breasts were still firm and her legs long. Surely he must have seen women with more buff bodies. With his looks and those eyes and that cock, he could have any of them that he wanted. Yet, he clearly wanted her--at least for the night.

When he stepped in front of her, only moments after circling her body, she gasped. "Mikhel! How...how did you get your clothes off so fast?"

For he was naked and fully, gloriously aroused. He had an absolutely beautiful body, but once she looked at his cock, she couldn't look away. It was large and thick, and extended from a dark mass of curls in front of his big, sculptured body as he held his arms out to her.

Sucking in her breath, she stumbled forward. He took her in his arms. His hard, hot cock pressed against her stomach. A rush of moisture trickled from her cunt and down her leg.

He tipped up her chin and looked down into her eyes. "My lovely Erica, I can smell your need for my cock." He bent his head and sensuously licked her neck. He pressed closer, gripping her hips in his hands. He rotated his groin against her, letting her feel the heat and weight of his thick cock. "Feel my need for your pussy and your blood, my Erica."

She shuddered, her legs trembling. She had to have that big, magnificent cock inside her cunt. Even if he killed her later, she would die happy. "You can have them both, Mikhel. Just make love to me."

Slipping an arm around her waist, he reached between their bodies and began rubbing the big head of his cock along the length of her cunt, testing her readiness for him. She bit her lip, closed her eyes, and held on to his broad shoulders, her whole body hit by countless waves of pleasure. Forgetting the condoms in her discarded shoulder bag, she thrust her hips forward, hungry for the first feel of his rock hard shaft.

He lifted her left leg across his hip, buried his lips against her neck, and propelled his hips forward, sending the head of his dick between the lips of her sex and into her already drenched channel.

Having her cunt invaded by the biggest cock she'd ever had made her leg buckle. She would have fallen, if not for the strong arm around her waist. Still kissing and licking her neck, he draped her other leg across his hip and slowly impaled her on the full length of his shaft. A jolt of heat and fire burned in her belly, quickly spreading to her stuffed pussy.

Oh, God, she'd never felt anything half as good. Gasping, she wrapped her arms and legs around him and began sliding up and down the length of his dick. She clenched her fingers in his hair, tore his mouth away from her neck, and greedily kissed his sweet lips. His tongue touched hers and in just a matter of moments, she shuddered to a blistering orgasm, soaking his still plunging cock.

"That's it, my love. Come for me, my Erica." As he whispered against her neck, he gripped her hips and began thrusting into her with rapid, powerful strokes that triggered another incredible climax. "That's it, my love. Cover my cock with your hot pussy juices. Come for me again."

"Oh, God, Mikhel…it's so good…your cock is so good…*oooh*."

Her cunt gushed until she felt weak. Moaning, she collapsed against him, burying her face against his shoulder, shaking with the aftermath of the absolutely blissful fucking she'd just received. Still on his feet, he held her in his arms, lightly kissing her hair. Although his cock was still buried to the hilt inside her, he no longer thrust into her.

Several moments passed before she lifted her head and looked up at him. "You didn't fall."

"What?"

"I've never had a man able to make love standing up without falling or leaning against something."

He kissed the tip of her nose. "You've never had a vampire make love to you."

"No." She leaned forward and kissed his lips. "I had no idea what I was missing, Mikhel." She sighed and drew her head back to look at him. "You are still so thick and hard. You haven't come."

"Not yet. I don't just want to fuck you, delicious though that was. I want to feel your warm blood running down my throat as I blast your sweet pussy full of my seed."

Her stomach muscles tightened and her pussy clenched impulsively around his thick, hard flesh. Oh, Lord, help her. The moment of truth had arrived. She licked her lips and looked into his dark eyes. "Couldn't you just...fuck me some more?"

"Oh, I intend to fuck you a lot more, but I need more. I need to taste your blood."

"Oh, God! I know I said you could have some, but I am so afraid."

"There's no need to be. I will not hurt you."

"I trust you, Mikhel," she lied weakly. She wanted to give him everything he wanted, but she *was* afraid.

"That's my Erica." Smiling, he walked over to the big bed. Somehow he managed to lower them both to the mattress, while keeping his cock firmly inside her. She lay on the big bed with him on top of her, between her legs. His eyes glowed and he bared his incisors as he slowly began to move his cock in her pussy.

Resting most of his weight on his extended arms, he rotated his hips. She gasped, feeling every inch of the thick, hot meat cleaving through her body, touching depths no man had ever touched before. The slow, controlled movement of his cock stirred glorious, indescribable feelings, not just in her cunt, but in every part of her body that could feel.

"Ooooh…*God*."

He used his knees to urge her legs further apart. He withdrew all but the big head of his cock from her clinging pussy, before lowering his weight onto her, crushing her breasts under his hard chest. Groaning softly, and burying his face against her neck, he shoved his shaft deep into her body. He then began a relentless fucking that shattered her universe into a series of endless, cataclysmic earthquakes, all centered within her burning, pleasure-filled cunt.

She came and came until she thought the ecstasy would kill her. Just as she thought she couldn't bear anymore, he sank his teeth into the side of her neck, cupped her butt in his big hands, and began drinking her blood. The combination of his cock and his teeth both assaulting her overwhelmed senses was too much. Shuddering with yet another orgasm, she moaned, and collapsed against the bed, feeling weak and exhausted. He clutched her to him, thrusting wildly, repeatedly into her until his come overflowed her pussy and trickled down her leg.

Finally, he lifted his teeth from her neck, withdrew his cock from her. When she muttered a soft protest, he cradled her body on top of his. He kissed her hair and stroked her shoulders.

"Oh, God!" She shuddered and pressed close to his big, damp body. "Oh, God, Mikhel! What was that?"

"It was bloodlust."

"I've never felt anything that good before."

"Neither have I."

"You haven't?"

"Not this good, no. " His voice sounded slurred. "Sleep now, my lovely Erica. When you wake, we'll love again. In the morning, we'll talk. Tonight, we make love again and again."

"Oh, God! Yes. Please. Yes!"

Chapter Three

Standing in the shower with cold water pouring over her, Erica closed her eyes and pressed her forehead against the wet tiles. In the light of morning, her recklessness of the night before was difficult to accept. Not only had she left the party with a man who had turned out to be a vampire, but she'd let him come in her unprotected pussy again and again. And now, instead of tearing out of his room while he slept, she lingered in the shower. Hesitant and pleased because she'd awaken that morning to find both nightstands covered with vases full of red roses.

Thank you for sharing last night with me. I will always treasure the memory of our first night together, as I hope you will. Happy belated birthday, my lovely, lovely Erica.

Mikhel, your bloodlust.

How could she ever be content with another man after having been loved by Mikhel? How could she ever forget him? Her pussy pulsed. Or that big, delicious dick of his?

Oh, Rica, don't be so dramatic. Okay, so he's a fantastic lover and made you feel like no other man ever has. You'll get over it. Get your butt in gear and get out of here. Now. She turned off the water, opened the shower door, and stepped right into Mikhel. "Oh!"

He stood just outside the shower door, naked and fully aroused. "Good morning, my beautiful Erica." Smiling, he slipped his arms around her and drew her close.

His cock throbbed against her. Ignoring the twitching in her cunt, she pressed her hands against his shoulders. "Mikhel. We can't. Not again."

He licked her neck. "Why not? Didn't I please you last night?" He rubbed his hips against hers.

She gasped, her body infusing with heat and lust. It took all of her willpower not to part her legs and give him easy access to her suddenly aching cunt. "You know you did."

"Then?" He touched a finger against her clit. "Do you want me to stop?"

"No," she admitted. She never wanted him to stop.

"Good. Because I can't stop." Grasping her hips in his hands, he pressed insistently forward. The tip of his cock sank into her.

A shock of desire ricocheted through her. She moaned and leaned her forehead against his shoulder. How could she resist him? "Mikhel. Please. I can't afford to get pregnant." Even as she spoke, her hips jerked forward and she greedily enclosed several more inches of his dick within the depths of her channel. Biting into his arm, she sank down onto him until his pubic hair meshed with hers. Lord, but he was thick and hard.

He tipped up her chin and looked down into her eyes. "It's a bit late to worry about that, my love."

"What…? What do you mean?"

"Just what you think I mean."

"I don't know what you mean, Mikhel!"

"We'll talk later, my lovely. Right now I have to have you."

She knew she should insist on an immediate explanation, but it was impossible not to respond physically to his luscious cock. Especially when he brushed his lips against hers and slowly began moving inside her. He rotated his hips, taking care to rub against her clit with each motion. Warm, delicious eddies of ecstasy chased each other around in her pussy.

"I need you to do something for me, my Erica," he whispered.

"Anything," she promised recklessly.

Keeping his cock in her, he drew his upper body away from her. He bared his incisors.

She sucked in her breath, her fear of him returning. "Isn't it too soon for you to take more of my blood?"

His dark eyes glowed and flickered. He brushed his fingers against her neck in a soft caress. "It's not your blood I want this time, my Erica."

"It's not?" She breathed a sigh of relief. "Good. Then why…"

"Let me show you." He put his right forefinger in his mouth. When he withdrew it, it was covered with blood.

"Oh, Mikhel! You're bleeding!" She instinctively reached for his hand. She brought his finger to her mouth and kissed it.

"That's nice. Will you suck it?" He asked softly.

"What?"

"Taste my blood, my Erica. Taste me."

A shock of revulsion went through her. She dropped his hand and stared up at him. "Suck…you want me to…drink your blood?" She would have pulled away, but he clamped an arm around her waist, keeping her body firmly joined with his.

"Yes. Taste me as I've tasted you."

"I can't!"

"Yes, you can." He bent his head and kissed her. She tried to keep her lips pressed firmly together, but the feel of his mouth, moving against hers, stirred emotions and passions she couldn't control. Her lips parted, and before she could stop him, he'd lifted his head away and pushed his finger between her lips and into her mouth.

She felt several drops of his blood fall on her tongue. Instead of making her gag, the taste of his blood burning in her mouth created a new sensation in her. Her revolution was quickly replaced by a need for more of his warm, sweet blood. This was what love, sex, and lust was all about: being filled with a vampire's cock while he bled in her mouth, filling her with his essence. Without conscious thought, she grasped his hand in hers and began sucking at his finger.

He stroked her hair while he slowly began to move his cock in her again. "Oh, yes. Yes, that's it, my Erica. Feel me. Suck me. Taste me. Share me."

She closed her eyes and sucked contently. Cupping one hand over his hard butt, she rotated her hips in time with his, eagerly matching him thrust for delicious thrust. His blood seemed to infuse a strange wildness in her. Her blood felt as if it were on fire. On some subconscious level she felt a sense of alarm, as if she were somehow being changed. She disregarded the slight sense of foreboding. Sucking his blood was too wonderful to be harmful if anyway.

When he suddenly withdrew his finger from her mouth, she cried out in protest and stared up at him. "Mikhel!"

He smiled down at her. "You're not used to sucking blood."

"I want more."

His dark eyes glowed. "Now you begin to see how addictive blood can be."

"Yes. Please give me just a little more."

"Not now, my love. Too much too soon and you'll get sick. In a day or two you can have just a little more. Let' go to bed."

She moaned in accent when he carried her back to the bedroom, never losing a beat of the piston like rhythm of his pumping dick. Lying on the bed under his big body, with his cock plunging into her with the force and speed of a jackhammer, she had one explosive orgasm after another.

She clung to him like a limp doll as he pumped her full of semen. When the world settled back on its axis, she buried her face against his shoulder, cupping a hand against his cock, which always seemed to be semi-erect. "Oh, Mikhel. That was so good."

"Fantastic," he murmured against her hair.

"Delicious," she countered, flicking the tip of her tongue against his nipple.

He laughed and hugged her close. "If we keep talking about how delectable it was, I'm going to need to do it again," he warned.

"Oh, no you don't, buddy!" She reluctantly pulled away. "What you need is a cold shower."

Still laughing, he allowed her to push him off the bed. "Okay. I'm going already."

After taking separate showers and eating a light breakfast, they spent the day sight seeing. Although Salem was only sixteen miles north of Boston, Erica had never visited The House of the Seven Gables or the enchanting Pickering Wharf. Strolling along the seaside harbor village, holding hands with Mikhel, she felt like a young girl in love for the first time. It didn't matter that the day was both cold and overcast.

Mikhel's frequent sidelong gazes and quick kisses left her feeling happy and carefree. For all she knew she might be pregnant, but what did anything matter as long as Mikhel was there, looking at her as if she were the most beautiful and desirable woman in the world?

The feeling of euphoria lasted until she and Mikhel parted after a late lunch. Standing alone in the ladies room, putting on fresh make-up, a sudden, abrupt chill ran up and down her spine. A feeling of menace seemed to envelop and surround her. Although she stood in front of the mirror and could clearly see that she was alone in the room, she turned quickly, looking over her shoulder. There was no one there.

Still, she bent and looked under all five-bathroom stalls. No feet were visible, but the feeling persisted. Taking a deep breath, she crossed the room and quickly jerked each and every stall door open. All were empty. She really was alone in the room.

She returned to the mirror, quickly applied her makeup, and hurried from the room, feeling as if some invisible danger pursued her.

Outside the ladies room, she paused, startled. A tall, dark man, dressed in all black, lounged against the opposite wall. For a moment, she relaxed, thinking it was Mikhel. "Damn but you look sexy as hell in black," she said. "Of course you look even sexier wearing nothing but your big, hard cock."

When the man straightened and looked directly at her, she found herself almost drowning in a pair of dark eyes that definitely did not belong to Mikhel. While she knew Mikhel could compel her with his liquid brown gaze if he chose to, she knew he wouldn't. This man seemed to have no such scruples.

Man? If he were exerting his will on her, maybe she was looking at another vampire, one without Mikhel's scruples. She could feel him reaching out to her. Almost overcoming her will.

She stood frozen as he allowed his dark gray eyes to make a slow, through inspection of her body. His gaze lingered on her breasts long enough to make her nipples harden before moving down to linger on her groin area. He made no effort to hide the fact that he liked what he saw.

To her surprise, this stranger's frank approval of her body was neither unwelcome, nor unpleasant. In fact, her pussy pulsed and the breath caught in her throat. God, she was becoming such an exhibitionist. First, she slept with a vampire, allowing him to seduce her into sucking his blood, and now she was enjoying being ogled by a strange man who looked even younger than Mikhel.

She cast a glance down at his leg and sucked in a deep breath. There was an unmistakable bulge of significant proportions lying against his leg. He looked as big and thick as Mikhel.

Mikhel. Mikhel. She was no longer on the prowl. She was with Mikhel. She gave a small shake of her head and started forward, her face hot with embarrassment.

For one moment, she thought the man would step in her path, but although he flashed her a knowing smile, he let her pass unmolested.

She rushed back to the main dining room. Still seated at the table they'd shared, Mikhel rose when she approached. His dark gaze searched her face. "What's wrong?"

Ashamed of her response to the stranger, she shook her head and slipped into the chair he held out for her. "Nothing."

To her surprise, he frowned and cast a swift gaze towards the exit leading to the ladies room. "Are you sure?"

She hesitated, bit her lip, and then decided to be truthful. Well, half truthful. "Actually, I'm a little rattled because there was a man waiting outside the ladies room when I cam out."

"And?"

"And he stared at me."

"And? You're a beautiful woman. You must be used to men staring at you."

She let that pass. "His staring didn't disturb me as much as how it made me feel."

"By that I suppose you mean excited or aroused?"

"Yes," she admitted, in a low, barely audible voice. "Mikhel, I don't understand what's happening to me. I don't go around hopping into bed with strange men."

He sighed. "And that's what you wanted to do with the man outside the ladies room?"

Thoughts of the size of the stranger's dick seemed seared in her memory. She nodded. "Yes, but I don't understand why. You've more than fulfilled my wildest fantasies. How can I want someone else?" She watched the tightening of his lips. "Please don't be angry."

He reached across the table and took her hands in his. "I'm not angry, but why you feel this way is something we're going to have to talk about — soon. "

"Why not now?"

"Trust me to know when the time in right?"

She shook off the feelings of dread and shame assailing her and nodded. "That's not my usual style, Mikhel, but all right."

He squeezed her hand gently. "You know what I am."

She lifted a hand and felt the puncture marks on her neck. "It's difficult to believe, but yes. I don't understand how—"

"Actually, I'm not a full-blood. My father is human, but my mother is a full-blood vampire, meaning both her parents were vampires."

"So how are you different from a full-blood?"

"In many ways. But for now I'll just say I'm different in that I'm nowhere near as fast, as strong, nor am I as driven by a need for blood."

"Mikhel, you drank my blood. For a while there, I was afraid you weren't going to stop until…"

He sighed. "I'm sorry you were afraid. I never want you to be afraid of me. Did I hurt you?"

She shrugged. "I don't know if it hurt or not." She smiled suddenly, licking her lips slowly. "If you remember, at the time, I was rather…preoccupied."

A brief smile touched his lips. "Believe it or not, I don't usually drink my lover's blood, no matter how aroused I become."

"But you have done it before?"

"Yes."

"Did you enjoy it?"

"No, not particularly. I'm not a full-blood so I don't usually hunger for my lover's blood."

"That's what I don't understand. If you didn't particularly enjoy it, why did I enjoy it so much?"

"I didn't enjoy it with the other women. With you, my enjoyment level went off the scale. But you and I are bloodlust partners. It makes all the difference. Any and everything we do together or for each other's pleasure, will be beyond sweet."

"So when you sucked your other lover's blood, have you ever gotten carried away and…"

"Drained a woman while making love to her, thus killing her?"

She nodded, not sure she wanted to know the answer.

"No. I told you, I don't usually mix the two. I've only done it twice before last night with you. Both times happened years ago and neither time was particularly memorable."

"Should I be flattered?"

"I don't know. Just know that you're very special. And I will never hurt you, my Erica."

She smiled. "I like the way you say my name and call me your Erica. I like the way you look at me. I like everything about you, Mikhel." She paused, remembering how the man outside the ladies room had affected her.

"Tell me, my tall, dark, handsome blood sucker, are there anymore like you at home?"

"I have a brother and a sister, Serge and Kattia, both younger and both apparent latents."

"Latents?"

"While they are undeniably stronger and faster than other humans, they have no other discernible vampire traits. Latents generally don't experience bloodlust."

"Bloodlust? You mean they don't drink blood?"

He hesitated. "They have the capacity to experience bloodlust, but for some reason, Mother says they generally don't. They also have sharpened incisors. As to whether or not they've used them…Serge is very…sexual."

"What does that mean?"

"If he's awake, he wants sex. Lots of it. All the time."

She smiled, running the tip of her tongue along her top lip. "He sounds a lot like you."

He grinned. "I only want sex all the time with you. I'm much more restrained with other women."

Did that mean he still wanted other women? She hardly felt in a position to ask. "So your brother and sister don't drink blood?"

"That's not what I meant by bloodlust. Bloodlust occurs when a vampire meets the perfect mate who spawns a lust, desire, and need, not only for blood, but for sex with that particular person. When the two desires are combined in the same person they create a need in the vampire to mate that overshadows everything else.

"It's during bloodlust that vampires are most fertile."

"You mean women vampires. Right?"

"I mean all vampires. Female vampires are more likely to get pregnant with their bloodlust and males are more likely to get their mates pregnant."

"What?" She blinked at him. "How…how much more likely?"

"Highly likely."

She bit her lip. "Mikhel…are you telling me I'm probably pregnant?"

"I don't know. I'm not a full-blood and I've never gotten anyone pregnant."

"And? I hear a but in your voice."

"But I've never been in bloodlust before."

She ran a hand through her hair. There was no need to panic. When she got back home, she'd go to her doctor and get a dose of morning after pills. "You could have told me all this *before* we had unprotected sex."

Tiny lights flicked in his eyes. "When I first saw you, I knew you were my bloodlust—the one woman who would create the perfect passion in me that all vampires live to experience."

The perfect passion? Okay. That explained what she felt for this man whose existence she hadn't even been aware of twenty-four hours earlier. One night spent with him and she found the thought of parting from him unbearable.

He lifted her hand to his lips and kissed her fingers. "There was no way I wanted anything between your pussy and my cock. I had to have full access to your pussy, my Erica."

"Oh, Mikhel. You are so smooth."

"No! I mean it."

She nodded. "I know. How is it that some lucky vampiress hasn't snatched you up by now?"

She found his noticeable hesitation unnerving. "Mikhel? Is there someone special in your life?"

"There's someone my mother would like me to mate with."

"Why?"

He shrugged. "Because she's a full-blood. My mother loves my father dearly, but she regrets that my brother and sister are latents and that I'm only a half-blood. If I mated with the full-blood as she wants, the Walker-Dumont line of vampires will not die off. If, on the other side, I father children with a human or even a latent, there's a high probability that our children would be human."

"And that would be a bad thing?"

He shrugged. "As far as my mother is concerned, yes."

"What about your brother and sister? Are they free to mate as they like or does your mother have mates lined up for them also?"

"Of course she has mates lined up for them. Rather or not Kattia falls in line with Mother's plans remain to be seen."

"And your brother?"

"Serge is young with a lot of life to live. He will do just as he always has: whatever he likes—whenever he likes, with little regard for the resulting consequences."

"So how do you feel about this full-blood your mother wants you to mate with?"

"She doesn't create a bloodlust in me. You do."

"But you mother won't approve of me."

"No, but then she doesn't have to. I approve of you. I want you. I need you. I won't give you up."

She smiled. "Oh, Mikhel! I'm so glad to hear that. I was wondering how I was going to forget you once I headed back to Boston."

His dark eyes glittered. "What makes you think I have any intentions of letting you go? Remember, I live in Boston too, Erica."

Just for a moment, she considered asking where this full-blood lived. But what did it matter as long as he didn't want her?

Chapter Four

They had dinner at a restaurant over looking the water again. Afterwards, he dropped her off at her hotel so she could check out. She would share his hotel room until they both returned to Boston in a few days.

Alone in her room, packing, Erica again felt an air of malice. As before, there was no one in the room with her. Remembering the incident at the restaurant that afternoon, she opened her hotel room door and looked out. She wouldn't have been surprised to see the stranger from the restaurant lounging in the hotel corridor, but it was empty. She closed the door and wedged a chair under the knob.

Moments after she finished packing, Mikhel called. "Are you ready?"

"Yes."

"I'll come up and get your bag."

"Thank you."

It was a relief to get in her car and follow Mikhel back to his hotel.

In his room, they undressed quickly. He lay on his back with his legs spread, fully aroused. Lord, but his cock was a thing of beauty. Feeling her cunt dripping just looking at him, Erica climbed onto his body, grasped his hot flesh in one hand and slowly impaled herself on him until she felt his balls against her buns.

He sighed softly and shuddered, trailing his big hands along her thighs and behind.

Smiling, she reached back to caress his balls and slowly began sliding her pussy up and down his thick, hot cock.

He closed his eyes and parted his lips in a soft, wordless sigh of pleasure, thrusting his hips up against her.

Watching the emotions ripple across his handsome face, incited her own passion. Closing her eyes, she increased the speed and frequency of her plunging hips. Suddenly, he gripped her hips in his hands and began bouncing her quickly up and down on him.

She gasped and bit her lip as her pussy began pulsing and contracting wildly around his cock. Lord, it felt good. Tendrils of pleasure erupted in her. Trembling, she fell against his chest, sucking his nipples and biting his neck as she came. Moments later, he blasted her full of his seed.

"Oh, Mikhel, if we keep this up without a rubber, I am definitely going to get pregnant," she moaned, kissing his lips.

He curled his fingers in her hair. "Would that be such a bad thing?"

Still impaled on his thick cock, she pressed her face against his shoulder. "I teach rich teenage girls at a very exclusive school. Showing up pregnant while unmarried is not an option."

He responded by kissing her. "Make love to me again, my Erica."

She lifted her head and stared down at him. "Now? Don't you ever get enough?"

"Have you had enough?"

"No," she admitted. They kissed and he rolled them over, so that she was on her back and he lay on top of her.

"Good, because I'm in the grip of bloodlust, my Erica. I need your pussy and your blood."

He began rapidly fucking his cock into her, pushing deep into her with each powerful thrust of his hips. Moaning and shuddering as the most delicious climax she'd ever experience detonated in her cunt, she mindlessly titled her head, exposing her neck.

She felt his teeth sink in. A jolt of electricity sizzled through her, as he fed at her neck while he came. When rational thought returned, she wrapped her arms around him. "Oh, Lord, I just know I'm going to get pregnant."

"Not to worry, my love. I'll take care of you both."

She was too tired to point out that she was perfectly capable of taking care of herself. She bit into his shoulder instead. "Next time, no condom, no pussy, buster," she warned.

"Yeah? What if I bribe you by letting you suck my blood?"

She shuddered in anticipation of tasting his blood again. "Let me suck your blood and you can have as much pussy as you want, whenever you want it," she admitted and drifted into a contented sleep.

* * * * *

Erica came abruptly awake. For several moments, she lay with her eyes closed. She savored the feel of Mikhel's warm nude body curled into her back, his big hands holding her as he slept. Then she felt the same sense of menace she'd felt earlier. She opened her eyes and lifted her head.

The moonlight shining in through the window provided the only source of illumination. She looked around the room, not really expecting to see anyone or anything there. After all, she'd been creeped out for most of the day. Her eyes widened and a soundless scream rose in her throat as she saw a pair of eyes glaring at her from a darkened corner.

Oh, god! It was the man from the restaurant. He was in the room with them. But it couldn't be. The eyes were too low. The man from the restaurant had been as tall as Mikhel. She was imaging things.

She snapped her eyes shut. There was no one there. She opened her eyes again, half expecting to see the dark, magnetic stranger. Instead, a small, dark woman with glowing eyes emerged from the shadows.

"Human whore! Mikhel is mine! You are about to learn the folly of tasting the cock that belongs to a full-blood!"

The woman's lips didn't move and Erica didn't know if she'd actually spoken the words or just projected them into her mind. Either way, she knew this woman was a vampire...the full-blood Mikhel's mother wanted him to mate with. And she meant to kill her.

She wanted to scream, to wake Mikhel, but she couldn't move or look away from the dark eyes that glowed with malice. Oh, God, she was about to die while Mikhel slept beside her.

Even as the thought formed in her mind, the woman became a dark blur, moving across the room so fast, Erica couldn't quite follow her movement. Now she stood over the bed, reaching for Erica's neck. And still she couldn't speak or move.

Before the small pale hands could close around her throat, she heard a low, angry growl. Mikhel's hands shot out and closed over the woman's wrists, wrenching her hands away from Erica's neck.

"Deoctra! Do not touch her!" Bounding up from the bed, he pushed out both hands, flinging the woman half way across the room.

Erica watched in stunned amazement as the woman spun around in the air and landed lightly on her feet. "You belong to me, Mikhel. I do not share what's mine with human whores. She has to die!"

Baring her incisors, she flashed back across the room, her malevolent gaze locked on Erica's throat. "Die whore!"

Mikhel leaped in front of Erica, crouching and growling. "Leave."

"Step aside, Mikhel."

"Never."

"This whore's ass is mine. Don't make me hurt you to get to her, Mikhel."

The woman's voice dripped with unmistakable venom. The sound of her voice, the confidence in her words filled Erica with a sense of fear she'd never known.

"Before you can hurt her, you will have to kill me, Deoctra!"

"No, Mikhel!" Erica reached out and touched his shoulder. "You don't have to fight for me. I'll go and I'll never come back."

"No! You are mine! I will never let you go." He hissed the words at her, without taking his gaze from the woman confronting him. "Stay back, Erica."

Stay back? While he risked his life trying to protect her? Not likely. She looked around the room for something, anything she could use against this woman she was certain could and would kill them both if she desired. The only thing she could see that might likely serve as a weapon were the bedside lamps that looked heavy enough to cause some substantial damage.

She snatched the nearest lamp off the nightstand, ignoring the sparks that flew as the cord tore away from the socket. Jumping off the bed, she put her back to the wall. She pushed the shade off the lamp, wrapped the cord around it, and held the base in both of her hands like a baseball bat.

Mikhel shifted his stance so that he crouched in front of her. "Stay out of this, Erica."

"I can't!"

Erica's heart thumped in fear when the woman, who looked about five feet tall and weighed in at about a hundred pounds, reached out and grasped Mikhel by the throat. She watched in horror as the woman lifted him off his feet and tossed him across the room. His head hit the wall with a loud thump and he slid slowly down to the floor where he lay, unmoving.

"Mikhel! No!" Rushing forward, Erica swung the lamp as hard as she could at the woman's head. Hissing and baring her teeth, the full-blood spun around and parried the blow with the side of a forearm. Then she ripped the lamp from Erica's hands and leaped at her, reaching for her throat.

Erica hit the carpet hard enough to jar her whole body. Before she could scramble to her feet, the woman's small, strong hands closed around her throat, immediately cutting off her air supply.

She rapidly overcame her first instinct: to try forcing the woman's hands from her throat. If Mikhel hadn't been able to do it with his superior strength, neither would she. Instead, she balled both hands into fists and slammed them against the woman's ears as hard as she could. At the same time, she jerked up her knee and rammed it between the woman's legs.

To her relief, the woman shrieked in rage and pain and released her. Gulping in deep, mouthfuls of air, Erica scrambled to her feet, snatched up the discarded lamp, placed her back at the wall, and crouched.

"Whore! I was going to kill you quickly. Now, I will slowly drain every drop of your blood from your body first! Your death will be very painful."

Thoughts of what this horror had done to Mikhel infuriated her. She knew she had no real hope of stopping this woman. She was going to die, but it was going to be *after* the goddamned fight. "Bitch! You want me? You come and get me!" she hissed.

The woman flew at her. Out of the corner of her eye, she saw a sudden blur of movement, then, Mikhel stood in front of her. Clasping both hands together, he swung at the woman. Although the dark head jerked back at the impact of the blow, the woman kept her balance. She leaped again and Mikhel reached out and grasped her throat in both hands.

Standing behind him, Erica saw the muscles in his back and shoulders tense as he lifted the woman off her feet and began shaking her. Erica sighed in relief and allowed her body to sag back against the wall. Her relief was short-lived. Bringing up her arms, the woman broke Mikhel's grip on her neck and spun away from him.

"Mikhel! Don't make me hurt you. You know you're not strong enough to stop me!"

"Don't count on that, Deoctra."

"The human whore has to die!" The woman flew at Mikhel, her lips drawn back from her teeth. She slammed her body into him, knocking him off his feet, against the wall next to Erica.

She immediately lifted the lamp in an attempt to club the woman. But the woman was no longer standing next to her. She was behind Erica, sinking her teeth in her neck. Although she was aware that she was about to die, every nerve in Erica's body seemed to fuse, making movement impossible.

"No!" Mikhel roared. "Deoctra, if you hurt her, I will kill you." Erica saw a fury and horror in his eyes as he lashed out at their tormentor, grabbing her by her neck, and physically wrestling her away.

Released, Erica collapsed against the wall, weakly pressing a hand against her neck in an effort to stop the blood that flowed from her wounds.

She watched helplessly as Mikhel and the woman tumbled around on the carpet, each clutching the other's throat. Icy chills seized her when the woman suddenly pinned him to the floor.

"You are mine, Mikhel. My bloodlust. If you won't come to me willingly, then I will take you forcefully." She exposed his neck. She then reached back to fondle his dick as she sank her teeth into his flesh.

"No. Please don't hurt him." Too weak to stand, Erica grabbed the lamp, and began crawling towards the middle of the room, where the full-blood fed on Mikhel.

There was a ripping sound and Erica realized the full-blood had torn her dress and panties away and was repeatedly lifting her hips up and slamming them down in an effort to impale herself on Mikhel's big cock.

But he wouldn't cooperate, twisting his hips from side to side so quickly that Erica could barely follow his movements.

"Let me have your cock, Mikhel. It's mine. Shove it in deep and hard. Let me have it all, Mikhel and I'll show you the ecstasy of fucking a full-blood's pussy!"

"No." Mikhel roared the word and Erica saw his hands shoot up and close around the woman's throat. His whole body tensed and he slowly, but steadily began to lift the woman off him.

Erica froze in terror as yet another small, dark woman suddenly appeared from the shadows near the struggling couple. Without looking at Erica, the woman reached down, grabbed the full-blood by her hair, pulled her off Mikhel, and tossed her across the room.

She hit the wall with a thud, but immediately bounded to her feet and spun to face the newcomer, her incisors bared. "Stay out of this, Palea."

The other woman bared her own incisors, her eyes gleaming with a fury that made Erica shudder. Oh, Lord, was this yet another full-blood who wanted Mikhel and was prepared to kill her to get him?

Chapter Five

"Deoctra, no one takes my son by force."

Son? Relief washed over Erica. This was Mikhel's mother, a full-blood. Even if she didn't approve of Erica herself, she clearly would not allow Deoctra to hurt him.

"He's mine, Palea. I have a right to take what's mine. He's fertile now. Surely you don't want him to mate with a human whore."

"It should be obvious to you that he's already mated with her. Several times. Her pussy is already full of his seed." Her nostrils quivered as she cast lightening fast gazes at Mikhel and then Erica. "Can you not detect the fragrant smell of their mating in the air?"

Cheeks burning, Erica cowered in the shadows.

Deoctra's eyes glowed and she screamed, touching her exposed cunt. "This is the pussy that should be full of his seed. Not some human whore. I will have what's mine, Palea."

"No one takes a child of mine by force. No one. Leave now before I kill you. If he's hurt…if you've subjugated his will, I will seek you out and kill you. Now go."

Deoctra turned angry, glowing eyes on Erica. "I'll take the human whore with me."

"You will not."

"Why not? Surely this human can mean nothing to you."

"She means enough to Mikhel for him to fight for her life at the risk of his free will. Leave now, Deoctra, or die now. The choice is yours. You choose to live a little longer. Yes?"

Erica sent up a silent prayer of thanksgiving when Deoctra moved into the shadows and disappeared.

The other woman turned to Mikhel. "My little one. You are all right? No?"

Mikhel struggled to his feet, and Erica's heartbeat returned to normal. "I'm all right, mother."

Palea Dumont rushed to her son and they embraced, kissing each other's cheeks.

Erica watched in amazement. Mikhel's nudity didn't seem to bother either one of them. Ashamed by her own lack of clothing, she pressed one hand over her mound and the other across her breasts.

Mikhel drew away from his mother and hurried across the room to kneel at her side. He touched her neck, then bent and kissed it tenderly. "My brave, beautiful, Erica! Are you all right?"

She nodded slowly, surprised. Other than being scared senseless and feeling weak, she seemed to be okay. She leaned forward and pressed her face against his shoulder. "What about you, Mikhel? Are you hurt? When she threw you across the room, I heard your head hit the wall and I thought…"

"Shhh. It's all right. I'm all right. I'm not so easily hurt."

"Now you tell me! Oh, Mikhel. I was so afraid."

He lifted her in his arms and carried her to the bed. He lay her on her back and pulled the sheet up to cover her breasts. "I know, but it's all right now."

She cast a quick look at his mother. "Cover yourself, Mikhel," she whispered. It was bad enough that the room reeked of sex and they were both naked. "Your cock is almost hard and your mother can see it!"

He shrugged. "It's not the first time she's seen it."

She gaped at him. "What? What do you mean it's not the first time? Are you saying ? Mikhel! I—what are you saying? Surely you and your mother…?"

"Oh, don't look at me like that, my Erica. I only meant that nudity is no big deal. We vampires are not bashful. My mother has seen my cock many times."

"Erect? Since you've been an adult?"

"Yes. When we're home, it's not usual for us all to be nude."

"All? Who's all?"

He shrugged. "Me, Serge, Kattia, my parents."

"You mean you all walk around naked and aroused in front of each other?"

"It's not a big deal, Erica." He turned to look at the woman who looked about twenty-five years old. "Mother, this beautiful, bashful woman is Erica Kalai…my bloodlust."

His mother emitted a low, soft sigh. "Oh, my little one. You didn't use protection. No? She's full of your seed and she's not even a latent. This is going to complicate things. You are sure?"

"I'm very sure, Mother."

"Think seriously, Mikhel. Do not be lead by lust alone. For all her faults, Deoctra can easily take your cock all night long. Yes?"

"So can my Erica." Then to Erica's dismay, he pulled the cover off her and settled himself between her legs.

"Mikhel!" She shoved against his shoulders, trying to push him off her. "What are you doing? Your mother's watching!"

"I know," he said softly. "She enjoys watching us make love." Holding her still, he sank his cock deep into her depths with one quick thrust.

The breath hissed from her throat. Her pussy caught fire and she pushed back against him, parting her thighs to give him easier assess. Even as she fought to keep from surrendering to the lust tightening her cunt, she clutched his butt in her hands.

"That's it, my lovely Erica. Take my cock and fuck me back."

Oh, what the hell. What if his mother was in the room watching? It was his mother. If he didn't mind her watching, why should she? She shuddered, surrendered completely to her desire, and began fucking back at him.

"Oh, God, Mikhel. Please fuck me."

"As often as you like, my love," he promised.

He picked her up and carried her to the writing desk in one corner of the room. He sat her on the end and thrust into her. Lifting her legs over his shoulders, she pressed her arms back to support herself and shoved her hips back at him. "Oh, Lord, your cock is so good."

"Then let me give you some more," he said and began fucking her with complete abandon.

Tossing her head back, she let the waves of bliss wash over her until they consumed her. Absolute paradise.

* * * * *

"Wake up, sleepy head."

Erica kept her eyes tightly closed and pulled the cover up over her face. She ached, she was tired, and she wanted to be left alone to consider the consequences of the mess she'd landed herself in. She still couldn't believe Mikhel had actually mounted her like that and fucked her while his mother watched with dark glowing eyes. Not that she was any better. She frowned. Or had his mother really been present? She was no longer sure. The night before was a blurred mixture of pleasure, terror, and confusion.

If she'd only stayed at the party with Nancy and Janna, none of this would have happened. "Go away."

The cover was firmly pulled down from her face and a pair of warm lips brushed against her mouth. "I'm sorry about last night. Forgive me for not doing a better job of protecting you."

So now he was going to pull the woe-is-me routine on her. Men. You couldn't live with them, but who the hell wanted to try living without them? She opened her eyes and blinked up at Mikhel, who immediately pulled the cover away completely and spread his nude body on top of hers.

Despite all the horror of the night before, her body immediately responded to his. But she was through being ruled by lust, that had nearly gotten them both killed. She pushed against his shoulders. "No, Mikhel."

He stared down into her eyes for several long moments before he groaned and rolled off her. She sat up and held the sheet against her breasts. "Is she going to come back, Mikhel?"

He extended silence was answer enough.

She shook her head. "Mikhel, you are very special. I've never met anyone like you and I know I never will again."

He sat up and looked at her, his dark eyes narrowed. "That sounds strangely like the beginning of a *Dear Mikhel speech*."

She nodded slowly. "It's been an incredible, memorable two days, Mikhel. I'm never going to forget you."

He shook his head. "Erica, I know last night was frightening for you and I'm sorry, but—"

"Mikhel, I was scared to death, not only for my own life, but for yours as well. I can't…I don't want to live like that."

He cupped his palm against her cheek. "You won't have to."

"How can I not when you can't guarantee that she won't come back?"

"She will come back," he admitted. "But you don't have to worry."

"Why not?"

His dark eyes began to glow. "Because I'm going to kill her when she does."

"Kill her? You mean…"

"I mean I'm going to kill her."

"No! Mikhel, she nearly killed you last night. If your mother—"

"She never intended to kill me nor did she almost kill me. In the first place, I'm not so easy to kill. I'm not a full-blood, but I am my mother's son as well as my father's. Granted Deoctra is a formidable opponent, but so am I. And I won't necessarily be facing her alone."

Oh, Lord! He expected her to help him. She still wasn't sure what had possessed her the night before to try to battle a vampire, but she was not about to try that again. She shook her head. "Mikhel, I adore you more than you could possibly know, but I can't…help kill her."

"Help?" He leaned forward and kissed the tip of her nose. "I didn't mean you, my love."

"Then who? Your mother?" She glanced around the room. "Where is she?"

"She's with my father."

"Then who?"

"If necessary, Serge will back me up."

"Your broth—but you said he was a latent with no real vampire tendencies!"

"Don't make the mistake of underestimating, Serge. Latent or not, he too, is our mother's son. He is very skillful in any and everything he undertakes. We're a close-knit family. Both he and Kattia will be there for me, if I need them. If necessary, Deoctra will die." He stared into her eyes. "You have to stay with me."

She shook her head. "I want to, Mikhel, but I can't."

"I have no intentions of letting you go."

She lifted her chin. "The choice is not yours, Mikhel. It's mine to make and I've made it. I'm leaving."

His eyes darkened. "You'll only leave if *I* let you. I could very easily force you to stay."

"I know you could." She shook her head. "But I also know you won't."

"Don't be so sure of that."

"I am sure of it. You promised me you wouldn't hurt me. Well, I'd consider forcing me to stay against my will hurting me. Are you suggesting that you lied when you said I could trust you?"

"No." He closed his eyes and leaned his forehead against hers. "I am not like Deoctra. I want you to stay with me because you want to be with me."

She kissed his lips and pulled away. "I do want to be with you. More than you could possibly know, but I have to go."

"Erica. Don't. Please. You have no idea what you mean to me."

"I know what you mean to me, Mikhel, but I can't go around dodging a killer vampire who wants me out of the way so she can have you. Please try to understand." She climbed off the bed and began pulling on her clothes.

He watched her in silence, his dark eyes glowing, his jaw clenching. When she finished, he turned onto his stomach and buried his face in the pillow. "Please, Erica. I'll kill her."

"I don't want you to kill her. I just want not to be afraid. I have to go." She leaned over and kissed his hair. "Please don't make this any harder."

"Go."

"What?"

He suddenly spun around and stared at her, his eyes dark and cold. "I said go! If you're going go!"

"Let's not part like this, Mikhel." She stretched out a hand to him.

He bared his incisors and sprang away from her. "Don't touch me. Just go!"

She snatched her hand back and lifted her chin angrily. "Oh, you're a real prince, Mikhel. One moment you're pretending you can't live without me, the next you're snarling at me as if you'd like to rip my throat out."

He leaped off the bed and confronted her, his eyes dark, forceful, and angry. "You don't want to know what I'm feeling right now. Just get out!"

There was undeniable menace in his voice and in the glowing eyes glaring down into hers. She was almost afraid of him, until she remembered his whispered promise that he would never hurt her.

She reached out a hand to caress his cheek. Although he bared his incisors, he didn't move away from her touch. "Leaving you is the hardest thing I've ever had to do."

"I told you not to touch me." He pushed her hand away. "Get out. Now!"

The words *while I'm prepared to let you go* hung unspoken in the air between them. She knew he walked a fine line between the need to force her to stay and the desire to allow her the freedom to make her own choice. Even as she backed away, she adored him even more for his refusal to force his will on her.

* * * * *

"If she means so much to you, why did you let her go?"

Mikhel turned from the window of his hotel room to face the man who lounged casually on the unmade bed where he and Erica had made love the night before. "I let her go *because* she means so much to me."

"All the more reason for forcing her to stay if you ask me."

He frowned. "You only say that because you don't know how powerful a force bloodlust is, Serge. How it drives and completely controls you."

"I'm inclined to think this bloodlust is more trouble than it's worth. When I meet a woman I want half as much you want your Erica, I'll keep her using any means necessary."

He frowned. "You sound like Deoctra. You don't force your bloodlust to do anything. If you have to use force, then she's not your bloodlust."

Serge picked up a pillow, held it close to his face and inhaled deeply. "I can smell her pussy on this pillow. She smells delicious."

"She is delicious."

Serge inhaled again before laying back, his face turned into the pillow. "What will you do if she doesn't come back?"

"I don't know," he said bleakly. He had never dreamed that having found his bloodlust he would ever lose her.

"Well, if you're not going to go after her and force her back, that means sooner or later she's going to get herself another man."

A low angry growl escaped his lips at the thought of his Erica with another man. He couldn't hurt her—no manner what she did. The man would be another story.

Serge sat up, his eyes narrowing. "If she doesn't come back, I'll go after her."

"No!"

"Yes. If you won't do what's necessary, I will."

He flashed across the room and stared down at his younger brother. "I won't have her hurt, Serge."

"Who's going to hurt her? Not me. Fuck her? Probably, but I'll bring her back to you unharmed."

He reached out and grabbed Serge by the throat. "Don't you touch her."

Serge pushed his hand away and rose to his feet. "It'll be me or some other man. At least I won't fall in love with her. I'll fuck her and bring her back to you."

"Stay away from her."

Serge's eyes narrowed. "That's not what I said when you fucked Lisa."

A memory flashed across Mikhel's mind of a tiny, brunette with wide, deceptively innocent blues eyes, huge breasts, and a tight, greedy pussy that had milked and sucked as much of his cock as she could take like he was her last fuck. Spending the night with her had been a decidedly pleasant experience.

"That was different."

"That's not what you said when you were fucking her."

He frowned. "She was not your bloodlust and you wanted to watch me fuck her. *She* wanted you to watch me fuck her."

"Yes, she did. And you did—until the poor woman could barely walk the next day. And I didn't complain. It's time to play fair, Mik."

"She's mine."

"And she'll continue to be yours. But fair is fair." Serge's dark eyes glinted. "Don't worry, Mikhel. I promise I won't fuck your Erica until she wants me to."

"She won't want you to."

"Has she sucked your blood?"

"Yes."

"And you can still say that?"

Mikhel took a deep, shuddering breath. He knew Serge had a point. But how was he supposed to share his Erica, his bloodlust with another man? Even Serge. He frowned. He had to get her back. Then he'd worry about how to keep Serge away from her.

"Serge, I am warning you!"

"I'll consider myself warned." Serge moved quickly across the room in time to avoid his halfhearted attempt to backhand him. "In the meantime, Katie and I will be next door if you need us." He paused at the door. "Don't worry, Mikhel. Even though I have every intensions of fucking her, given the chance, I won't fall for her. Although she's pretty, she's entirely too blond and too fair for me. As you know, I like my women much darker."

He nodded slightly. He'd known of Serge's preferences for quite a while, which was why the tiny brunette had surprised him. He dismissed the sudden, unexpected thought that he'd like the opportunity to spend a night or two with the woman Serge finally settled down with.

"Have you told mother yet?"

Serge shook his head. "No."

"Why not?"

"She's already upset about you and your Erica. Why should I give her more grief, especially since there's no one special? Well, not exactly."

"You have someone in mind?"

Serge's eyes seemed to glaze over and Mikhel knew his mind was far away. "Yes. The woman from Philly."

"The woman from…what woman from Philly?" Mikhel frowned. "Not our client, Serge. We were hired to provide security for her, not romance her."

"I intend to do both."

"Why choose her?"

"I don't know about bloodlust, Mik, but the first time I saw her, I knew she was someone special who I wanted to spend a lot of time with."

"And how does she feel?"

"I don't know. I haven't approached her yet."

"Why not?"

Serge shrugged. "Unlike your delicious, uninhibited Erica, she is not likely to succumb so easily…unless I use coercion."

He leveled a finger at Serge. "Do not imply that Erica is easy."

Serge grinned. "Oh, but that's what I'm counting on."

"Well, she's not. You just worry about your woman when you get another one. You're the last person I thought would have a problem with coercion."

"Normally I wouldn't and don't have a problem with it, but this woman is different. I want her to want me."

"Ah. You begin to understand the allure of a woman who wants you."

"I suppose."

"Good. In the meantime, leave her alone. Business is business. Find your pleasure somewhere else."

Serge shook his head. "If you don't want to mix business with pleasure, don't. But don't try to dictate to me, Mik. You should know by now that it won't do any good. There is no way I'm going to stay away from her."

"So you intend to play around with a client and then just walk away?"

"Why not?"

"It's unprofessional. Besides, Mother won't be pleased."

Serge grinned. "Ah, well. There's always Katie."

After Serge had gone, Mikhel turned back to the window. Where was his Erica? He closed his eyes, straining to 'feel' her through the tenuous connection that had started to form between them.

Erica. Erica, my love. Come back to me.

Chapter Six

Erica fought back tears as she road the elevator down to the ground floor. Every time the elevator door opened, she struggled off an almost overpowering need to run back to Mikhel. Leaving him had been the only practical thing she could do. She was not going to stay with him and spend what would undoubtedly be the rest of a very short life, trying to avoid being killed by the likes of Deoctra. And the Lord only knew how many other full-bloods might be lusting after him.

Tossing her suitcase into the trunk of her car, she drove out of the hotel parking lot, heading for home and sanity. Forgetting Mikhel would be impossible, but time would heal the newly self-inflicted wound in her aching heart. How dumb was she anyway to fall so hard for a man after spending just two nights with him?

So he was a fantastic lover who looked at her as if she were the only woman in the world. She'd found him and she'd find another handsome hunk with a big, hard cock that felt so very delicious inside her. In time, she might even meet a man like the one outside the ladies room. Hopefully, the man in question would be older.

She might meet a man with a big cock, she conceded. But no manner how big his cock, he wouldn't be Mikhel. And that was the problem. A scrumptious shiver of remembered pleasure rushed up and down her spine. It wasn't just that he was handsome and had a really large dick. Granted that had been the basis of the initial attraction. But it wasn't the size of his dick that made her heart feel as if it were breaking. It was the sense of wonder and belonging she felt when with him. The knowledge that he wanted her so badly that his desire for her kept his dick in a perpetual state of arousal, the certainly that he considered her his soul mate. No. His perfect mate. His bloodlust. Damn it. She was his bloodlust. And he was hers.

What good would living to a ripe old age be if she did it without Mikhel? What good was anything without him? Okay. So Deoctra might kill her before Mikhel could stop her. But that was a chance she was going to have to take, because damned if she'd let that full-blood bitch stand between her and Mikhel.

Fifteen minutes away from Boston, she turned the car around and headed back to Salem. The twenty minute return drive to Mikhel's hotel seemed to last an eternity. What if he were already gone? Or what if he didn't want her anymore? What if she walked in and found him fucking Deoctra? Then the bitch would have to die!

Her eyes filled with tears of relief when she spotted Mikhel's car in the hotel parking lot. He was still there. Barely taking the time to lock her car, she ran into the hotel and jumped on the first elevator going up.

Outside his room door, she pushed the *Do Not Disturb* sign aside and fumbled in her shoulder bag until she found the keycard he'd given her. She swiped it through the lock, pushed the door opened, and rushed into the room.

Still naked, Mikhel turned from the window, his incisors bared. She closed the door and leaned back against it, swallowing several times to moisten her dry throat. She waited for him to smile and rush across the room to take her in his arms. He remained where he was, his lips pressed together in a grim line.

"I came back," she said after an extended silence.

"Why?" He glanced around the room. "Did you forget something?"

Cute. He was going to make her beg. Okay. She could do begging. She kicked off her shoes and started across the room, undressing as she went. She stopped in the middle of the room, clad only in her silk underwear. "Yes. You."

Although his eyes began to glow and his cock stirred, he stayed where he was. Oh, he was definitely going to make her beg. "Okay, you want me to beg?"

He shrugged. "You made me beg when I asked you to stay and then you left anyway. It only seems fair that you beg now. You do that and maybe I'll consider taking you back."

"What?" She lifted her chin. "You want me to beg? In your dreams, buddy!" She unhooked her bra and stepped out of her panties. "I'm not begging for what's mine." She pointed to a spot in front of her. "If you know what's good for you, you'd better get your hard butt over here. Now. Don't make me come and get you."

The words were barely out of her mouth before he flashed across the room and stood in front of her. "Why have you come back?"

"Because I couldn't stay away." She bit her lip. "Don't you...want me?"

"Nothing's changed. I am who I am, Erica. I am what I am."

She nodded. "I know." She caressed his cheek. "And I adore who and what you are."

"Are you sure you know what you're doing, Erica, in coming back here? If you stay now, I can't guarantee that I'd be strong enough to let you leave again if you change your mind."

"Mikhel, I can't promise what I'll do in the future, but I'm here now. Isn't that enough?"

"For now."

"Now is all we have, Mikhel."

"No, my Erica. We can have almost all the time we want together. There are things about us that you can't possibly imagine."

Therein lay part of her fear. "I can't think beyond now. This moment." She moved her lips against the fine, dark hair on his chest. "I am *your* Erica, Mikhel. Your bloodlust." She lifted her head and looked up at him. "And you are mine."

His chest expanded as he took a deep breath. "I have waited my whole life to meet you."

She smiled as he lifted her in his arms and carried her across the room to the bed. "Your whole life? Mikhel, you're only thirty."

He sat on the side of the bed, staring down at her. "There's something I need to tell you about that."

"What?"

He sighed. "Actually…I'm not thirty."

"Oh, Lord." She sat up. "I knew it! Please don't tell me you're in your twenties. I knew you didn't look thirty. How much am I robbing the cradle by?"

He leaned forward and kissed her cheeks. "Actually, I'm a lot older than I look." He drew back. "I'm sixty."

"Sixty? There's no way you're sixty!"

"But I am. As a half-blood, I age much slower than a normal man would."

"Even so you…oh, damn!" She linked her arms around his neck. "I don't care how old or young you are. You are mine." She reached down and fondled his dick and balls. They felt warm and hard. "And I want what's mine."

She lay back on the bed and parted her thighs. "Now."

Cupping her breasts in his big hands, he leaned forward and feathered her lips and neck with kisses. "My beautiful, adorable, Erica. I need your pussy and your blood. There's a hunger inside me . . . inside my soul, my heart…my cock, that only you can fully and truly satisfy."

She shuddered and buried her face against his neck. "Stop talking," she told him. "And put that big, lovely dick of yours where it belongs—in my aching cunt."

He pulled back and grinned down at her. "Oooh. Dirty talk. I love it." He spread his big body out against hers and slowly began to kiss her, running his hands over her body.

Moaning, she pressed closer. "Mikhel, please. I'm on fire and my pussy is already soaking wet. Skip the foreplay and give me some cock."

He laughed and lightly nipped one of her breasts with his teeth. "Cock coming up, my Erica." He turned her so that they were both on their sides, with his body curled against her back.

She felt his hard dick against her buns and pushed back at him. Lifting one of her legs, he pressed forward, sending his entire length deep within her quivering pussy with one forceful stroke.

She moaned, shuddered, and closed her eyes as a thrill of delight spread out from her cock-stuffed pussy to surge through her whole body. He slipped one hand around her waist to rub against her clit, while the other one, caressed and massaged her breasts. Then he began to fuck her senseless, relentlessly pounding his big cock deep within the walls of her cunt. He seemed bigger and thicker than usual, stretching and filling every centimeter of space within her climaxing cunt. The sensations emanating from her pussy were absolutely incredible. Oh, Lord. How could anything feel so wonderful? So devastating? So heavenly?

There was only one way this could get better. "Oh, Mikhel. You have my pussy. Take all of me. Suck my blood. Fill me with your seed while I fill you with my blood."

She clutched at the arm across her waist and titled her neck. Growling softly in his throat, he bit gently into her flesh. As she felt the blood flowing out of her body and into his mouth, her pussy…her body…the universe exploded around her.

Groaning and straining, he suddenly rolled them over so that she lay on her stomach. Lying on top of her with his incisors still buried in her flesh, he shuddered and came, pumping her so full of his seed that it overflowed her cunt and ran down her leg.

Even after he came, he held her still under him. Rotating his hips, he pumped his hard thick length deep in her, piston like. She sank her teeth in the bed sheet, her hands clenched at her sides. His deep, hard thrusts hurt like hell, making her cunt burn. But Lord, it was such a sweet, sweet pain. She moaned and came again. Finally, he withdrew his teeth from her. Long after his body stopped shaking, he gradually pulled his cock out of her sore channel, and lay behind her. He licked the last drops of blood from her neck and stroked her body, whispering to her. *She was beautiful. She made him happy. She was his.*

"I'll bet you say that to all your human whores," she teased drowsily.

He laughed softly. "Hardly. You are the first human woman I've met who could take all my cock without asking me to stop, slow down, or take some of it out."

"I can sympathize." She rubbed her sore pussy. "I've never had such a large, hard cock in me before. For a while there I felt as if half a baseball bat was being rammed into me."

He stiffened behind her. "Half a baseball bat? Oh, damn. That sounds unpleasant. I hurt you. I'm sorry. I—"

"Don't be. It did hurt near the end. How could it not at the speed you were shoving into me? For a while there, I thought you were going to poke a hole in me. But damn, I loved it."

He buried his lips against her neck. "I'm sorry," he said again. "I tried to hold back. I did, but you have no idea how good it feels to be able to plump my entire cock inside you. Just to be able to make love to you without holding back is so incredible. When we make love, I feel as if your pussy was custom made for my cock. But I promise I'll be more careful next time."

"Don't you dare." She wiggled her buns against his thighs. "Seems I like it a little rough. At least I do with you. Lord, there's nothing as exquisite as feeling my pussy slowly being stretched to capacity by your big, thick cock."

"Stretched to capacity, huh? And you like that? Sounds a little kinky to me."

"Oh, yeah? You're a fine one to talk about kink. Sucking your lover's blood is the ultimate kink."

"Depends on what neck of the woods you hail from." He laughed. "Pun intended. Where I come from it's not kinky."

She turned her head and kissed his lips, stroking her hands over his tight, hard thighs. "Kinky or not, that was so good. Tell me, Mikhel, are all vampires as well hung as you?"

He nipped her neck. "For your information, the size of my cock has nothing to do with being a half-blood."

"Are you sure? I don't know that I've ever met a man with such a...big, thick dick." She dismissed an insistent memory of the man outside the ladies room.

"If you think I'm big, wait until you see my brother and father."

She pushed her elbow against his ribs. "I can imagine no occasion when I'll see your brother or your father's cock!" She bit her lip, then letting her curiosity get the better of her, she asked, "You mean they're bigger than you are?"

"Yes. Serge is thicker and longer by an inch or two, but my father is what my mother calls hung like a horse."

She shuddered, remembering his mother's tiny stature. "Your poor mother."

"On the contrary, from the way she cries out blissfully every time they make love, I think it's safe to assume that she loves every inch of my father's cock."

"Mikhel! How can you talk so casually about your parents' sex life?"

"I told you. We're a very uninhibited lot."

"Just how uninhibited are you?"

He stirred against her. "I don't want to scare you off."

"Mikhel! I want to know what I'm getting into."

He sighed. "Okay. Sometimes we make love together."

"We?" She half rose. "What do you mean by together?'"

He pulled her back down against him. "There's no need to sound so outraged. We don't engage in incest, but we do sometimes watch each other make love."

She sat up and turned to look down at him. "You watch your parents making love?"

"Sometimes."

"You mean you actually watch your father put his cock in your mother's…in her…?"

"I think the word you're looking for is pussy," he said, sounding amused. "And the answer's yes. As you know she's small and fragile looking. He's big. It's an incredible turn on to watch his huge cock disappear into her—"

"Okay." She sank back down against him. "We've reached the too much information stage." She blew out a deep breath. "Mikhel, how can you watch your parents make love?"

"We don't watch when they make love. That's private. We only watch when they fuck during a Family Fuck Fest."

"A what?"

"A Fuck Fest. Vampires have them all the time. In addition, we have family only ones. It's when we all get together and make love in one room. It's an incredible experience."

"And you actually call them Family Fuck Fests?"

"Why not? That's what we do during them. Years ago, when I was younger we used to call them Love Fests, but Serge began calling them Fuck Fests and somehow the name stuck."

A Family Fuck Fest. Lord, something was happening to her because the idea of a Dumont Family Fuck Fest sounded so damned intriguing. "Make love…Fuck Fest…whatever you call it, Mikhel, watching your parents…together is beyond kinky."

He gently bit into her neck. "It's uninhibited and exciting. As you'll see."

A mental picture formed in her mind of a vampire orgy. Willing women having their pussies and other openings drilled by handsome, magnetic vampires with huge cocks. The idea of watching the couple responsible for Mikhel's birth fucking each other was extremely erotic. Her pussy tingled at the thought.

"I'll reserve my judgment," she said primly.

"No, you won't." He licked at her neck and slipped a finger inside her. "I know the thought excites you, my beautiful Erica. I can feel you creaming around my finger and I can smell your excitement."

"You vampires and your damned sense of smell." She laughed and kissed his arm.

He lazily rubbed his thumb against her clit. "There's a whole world of new experiences awaiting you, my lovely Erica."

Something in his tone gave her pause. Just maybe all the experiences wouldn't be pleasant. But she'd worry about that later. "Nothing too drastic, I hope."

"You might find some of our customs hard to understand at first, but please know that no matter what, you're my bloodlust."

She was definitely not going to like everything ahead of her. But she was held hostage by her feelings for him. "Oh, Mikhel, I was a fool to think I could ever bear to give you up."

He nuzzled her neck. "Never fear, my lovely Erica. I have no intentions of giving you up. Ever. You are mine. Forever."

"Forever," she echoed.

She had no idea how she was going to explain him to her family and friends. But she'd worry about that later. It was as she drifted off to sleep that she remembered Deoctra. The Lord only knew when that full-blooded bitch would turn up again or how they would handle her. Or if they could handle her.

Mikhel's arm tightened around her waist suddenly. "It's all right. Sleep without fear, my Erica," he whispered. "Deoctra won't catch me knapping again."

His words startled her. She lifted her head and looked into his eyes. "But…how did you know what I was thinking?"

He stared into her eyes. She felt as if he were looking into her soul, stripping away everything but her feelings for him. "You have a lot to learn about vampires, my Erica. I've tasted your blood and filled you with my seed. You've tasted my blood. That's created a bond between us."

"Are you telling me you can read my mind?"

"Would it bother you if I could?"

"Yes! Mikhel, my thoughts are my own! I said I wanted you in my bed, not in my head."

He grinned at her. "Then I'm not telling you that."

"Mikhel!"

"Okay. I can't read your mind, but I can…sense some of your feelings and it's only natural you should be worried about Deoctra. But don't. I'll be ready for her. The next time she shows up, she won't like her reception."

She settled back against him, closing her eyes. She was probably going to need all the sleep she could get. With a vampire lover whose mother didn't approve of her, and a full-blood who wanted her dead, she had a feeling her future was going to be fraught with major surprises and danger. But with Mikhel as her bloodlust, it would also be filled with contentment and joy beyond compare. She had to trust that it would be an equal trade off.

"Let the bitch come," she told him with a bravado she didn't fully feel.

"I know you're afraid, my love, but I'd willingly die to protect you."

"I know and I trust you." She reached back and caressed his semi-hard flesh. "You are mine and I intend to keep you. She's not getting any of this cock. My cock."

"Your cock, my Erica," he echoed, his voice a low, satisfied murmur.

About the author:

Marilyn Lee welcomes mail from readers. You can write to them c/o Ellora's Cave Publishing at P.O. Box 787, Hudson, Ohio 44236-0787.

Also by Marilyn Lee:

- Bloodlust
    - Things That Go Bump In The Night
    - The Taming of Serge Dumont
    - Forbidden Desires
    - Nocturnal Heat
- Branded
- Breathless In Black
- Carnal Confessions
- The Fall of Troy
- Full Bodied Charmer
- Pleasure Quest
- Shifting Faces
- The Talisman
- Moonlight Desires

A Little Too Charming

by Treva Harte

Well, this wasn't much fun.

Janna tried to look upbeat rather than tired. After all, Lori had probably gone to a lot of trouble for this party. Everyone else seemed to be having a good time. In fact, they were having such a good time that Janna had no one to talk to. Erica was dancing—or something—with some luscious guy in a Dracula costume. They looked more like they were trying to have sex on the dance floor.

That was one lucky man. Janna knew Erica was crazy about vampires. How many times had she dragged Janna and Nancy to see the local Dracula film festival? Janna's brain had checked out about the second time she saw Bella Lugosi. On the other hand she had to admit Frank Langella had his moments…

Stifling a yawn at the thought of those hours at the movies—or maybe because she'd had about five hours' sleep last night followed by a flight home—Janna searched the room for other people she knew.

Nancy had been around a little while ago, but now she'd disappeared. Janna was dying to know how she'd managed to transform her mousy image to that of warrior-goddess while she'd been in the little witch's room, but probably some goblin of the masculine persuasion had scooped her up and carried her off.

Erica waved happily at Janna as she headed for the door with her caped dance partner. It looked like Erica's birthday was going to end with a bang. Definitely.

Fine. Good for both her friends. She'd come to this party to be with them and they were gone. Right now Janna would give anything to go to bed—alone—and have some catch-up sleep. Unfortunately, that just wasn't going to happen.

She thought she saw Paul dressed as a pirate and debated heading for the food table and out of sight. Paul had been less than understanding when she told him she had work that would take her out of the country for several weeks. Things hadn't been going so well before that—she'd been much too busy to try to work on their potential relationship. Anyhow. She wasn't sure who had dumped who, but they were definitely not even remotely a couple anymore.

Janna glanced at her watch and sighed. She could stay about another half hour, but what was the point? She might just as well get her work over with and then go back home. You couldn't connect with people in thirty minutes when your mind was mulling over how to talk to a potential new recruit. A potential new witch recruit, at that.

All Fred had told her was that they had to sign on the guy. And that he was a witch. Could guys even be witches? It didn't matter. You didn't argue with the vice-president of your ad agency.

"So now I have to pretend to be interested in all this stupid black magic mumbo jumbo," Janna muttered.

When you lived in Salem you heard more than enough about witches. Janna was sick of hearing about them. If only Salem really had gotten rid of them when the town had the chance!

Well, might as well get work over with. It was close enough to their appointment. Janna went to the kitchen, called a cab, and headed for the door. The place was so crowded by now that she couldn't even find Lori to thank her before she left.

She almost fell over an old woman as she went down the stairs. The woman mumbled something about love. Love was hers? Janna couldn't see too well in the sudden darkness, but the woman was probably some poor crazy street person who made no sense at all.

Janna walked a little faster toward the cab. Poor crazy woman or not, there had been something just a little creepy about that encounter. You just never knew what might happen.

"Look for the truth inside!" The woman suddenly yelled after her, quite clearly.

"Inside what, for heaven's sake?" Janna scowled and turned her attention to the cabdriver. "Oh no, I didn't mean you. I need to get to—" She looked at the address she'd scribbled down— "Derby Street."

Wonderful. She'd hang out with the witch-hunting tourists for Halloween. It figured that Treadwell Grimes would have his shop there. Just why he would want to see her there at this ungodly hour was beyond her.

For a moment she thought about whether he planned to hit her on the head and have his evil way with her. Oh yeah. She should be so lucky. No one had bothered to have their evil way with her in far too long. Besides, more practically, nearly everyone in her agency knew where she was heading for tonight. She was perfectly safe.

Janna massaged her forehead. If she'd just had a little more time, she'd have done some proper research on this guy. Fred had shoved this assignment at her the second she'd been stupid enough to walk in the office door. She should've just waited until tomorrow to show up at work.

At least she knew something about the business that wanted to use this Grimes person. She could talk up what a great company they'd be to work for and how very, very solvent this corporation was. Even witches must care about money.

She felt her eyes shutting. No. She couldn't go to sleep. It wasn't that far…

* * * * *

He slicked his hair back with one hand, hating the betraying gesture. He wanted to impress her. She had no idea who he was or what she'd come to mean to him, but he was going to change all that. Had to change all that. He'd never wanted to impress any woman in his life. He'd never needed to.

He pushed his creation into the oven and turned the dial. Usually he enjoyed cooking, but not tonight.

This was a fine time to get nervous.

"C'mon. You're fucking charming. Every woman you've ever met has told you that. Charm her, you idiot."

Wonderful. Now he was talking to himself.

Suddenly his skin prickled. That must mean she was near.

Hastily he flicked off most of the lights. They needed to start in the dark.

* * * * *

What evil spirit have you familiarity with?
None.
Have you made no contract with the devil?

No.

"You sure this is where you want to go, ma'am?"

She woke up with a start, feeling panicky. Oh, no. Now she was nodding off in strange places, having nightmares and still not getting any rest. She'd been having some awful dreams lately.

Janna resolved to finish up this business and get home fast while a few brain cells still functioned. When she was home, in her own bed, the nightmares would stop. Probably.

Then the driver's question registered. She stared out of the cab and looked up. Janna could see why the driver sounded hesitant. The tiny shop was dark except for what looked like a candle in the upper floor's dormer window.

"This is the address." Janna glanced at the paper again to make sure. "Would you do me a favor and wait until someone lets me in before you leave?"

Would it be just too perfect if the guy had gone home and forgotten all about her? Janna smothered a nervous giggle. Maybe he'd gone trick-or-treating. It was almost disappointing when she knocked on the door and heard a muffled voice call "Coming!"

She waved the cab driver on. As the taxi drove away she waited, listening to the sounds of footsteps clattering down the stairs. At last the door opened. A large presence loomed at the entrance. Janna opened her mouth to say hello and found herself pushed against the door.

A very warm mouth covered hers and took advantage of her opened mouth to press a very agile tongue inside. Oh my God! Janna pushed against some very broad shoulders in a sudden panic. They were in public, for heavens' sake, right on the front steps of his store. Anyone could walk by and see them. This was a bad idea. Probably. On the other hand, that tongue was very persuasive. She knew she shouldn't, but she felt herself relaxing into that unknown body and mouth. The mouth and tongue seemed to have no intention of ever stopping.

Before long she found herself returning that kiss. She didn't even know what her partner looked like, but she could tell he was strong and tall and, oh yes, an excellent kisser. Stunned, Janna realized she'd gone from pushing at his shoulders to clutching them. She felt warm. Really warm. Maybe she'd been without a guy a little too long, maybe that mouth was a little too good, but she didn't care. This mystery shadow-man's kiss was lethal.

His leg expertly nudged her own legs wider and then she could feel just how glad he was to see her. Janna knew she had to stop. This could be dangerous. This was way too much.

Hmmm. He felt like way too much. She was insane. She was in lust. It was long and strong and—

She rubbed herself against that fascinating cock. Janna heard herself making an appreciative noise deep in her throat. She didn't want to stop. She wasn't sure she could stop.

A light switched on by the door.

"Oh." He leaned against the door.

Oh? That's all he could say? Then Janna's eyes adjusted to the light.

Oh.

Oh wow. Oh blessed Jesus wow.

Fred hadn't bothered to mention this guy was gorgeous. Tall, long black hair to his shoulders with blue eyes for a contrast to his otherwise dark good looks. He might be a little young. She hoped he wasn't under twenty-five, though he might be. Oh well. She had no prejudices against younger men. Not in the least. She bet this one had lots of stamina.

He had a killer smile too.

Fred had proven he was an advertising genius once again. This guy would make a camera sit up and sing to all those potential customers out there.

Or maybe she was dreaming a very good dream this time.

"Well, uh, hello," Janna managed. "You know, I didn't quite realize until you grabbed me what you meant when you said you were coming."

That ought to get his attention. Oh yeah. After trying to gobble up the man's mouth, what could be a more sophisticated line than that?

His smile broadened from welcoming to what looked like genuinely amused. He had a dimple. Just one. On his left cheek. Yum, yum, yum.

"I'm sorry. I thought you were someone else. No matter. Greetings." He stepped back as if to get a good look at her. "I'm very happy to meet you at last, Janis."

All those warm, tingly feelings dissipated. Poof! Janna scowled. "I'm not Janis." She hadn't been Janis since she was about five and announced that Janna was what she wanted to be called instead. Janis was so ordinary.

Even worse, this clod couldn't know that had been her name. He'd just forgotten her real one. First he'd thought she was someone else and then he mixed up her name!

"Whatever you prefer." She could almost see his mental shrug.

"I prefer my name, thank you, Treadwell."

"Ted."

"Oh? Well, I suppose I have to go with whatever *you* prefer—" Janna bit her lip. She had to get a grip. No matter how much she loved to win an argument, she was supposed to be charming. She was supposed to talk him into signing onto the team.

Janna tried smiling back instead. That was a start. People had told her she had a cute smile. Right now she would have preferred a come-hither smile or a sex-bomb smile but she had to make do with what she had.

She thought about her outfit and mentally groaned. When she had first grabbed the long black T-shirt and tights and decided to dress as a witch, she figured she could get away with it for a night that combined a costume party and a business appointment with a witch. Now she wondered if maybe it was a little too short or that it looked too baggy or…

"I didn't expect you to look so good." The guy's voice was wonderful. He had this lovely deep rumble of a voice. "If you don't mind me mentioning how good your legs look in that attire."

Should she mind? Probably. This was business after all. Instead Janna smiled again and decided not to say anything.

Right. Business. "This is short notice for me, Ted, but I do have some reasons I've put together on why you might want to become a spokesman for Charms Unlimited." Janna launched into her pitch.

Ted shook his head. "No."

"No?" She almost squeaked out the words. She'd come all the way out here on Halloween for heaven's sake and she didn't even have a chance to try to sell this guy?

"I mean I don't want to talk business this minute." He beckoned her further inside. "You need to sit down and relax a minute. Have something to drink. You look tired enough to fall down."

"Oh." Janna realized they were still standing in the entrance to his shop. Perhaps she had been a little abrupt. Janna knew she needed to get herself together. She needed to impress this guy. Why did she feel all off balance tonight? Other than being kissed senseless, of course.

"I don't really need anything more to drink. I just left a party. Between the drinks there and jetlag I'm already in bad shape."

"I see. In that case, come here and hold my hand."

He held out his hand and, a little stunned, Janna put her hand in his. Then he began to lead her through the dark hall and up the stairs.

"I think I've blown a fuse or something worse," the man told her. "Only half the place seems to want to let me use electricity. I fiddled with the fuse box but nothing responded. I need to guide you upstairs. The steps are old and steep and I don't want you to fall."

His hand was strong and big and very touchable. Why should she care why she got to hold it? No. No, she should care. This guy showed every indication of being a sex maniac.

But it was such a nice hand. And there were so many other, um, nice things about him. Besides, he was right. The stairs were steep. Once or twice she had to hang on to that hand for balance.

"Here we are," he said, cheerfully. He lit another red candle and placed it on the kitchen counter. It added a bit more light to the candle in the window.

Janna blinked. He lived up over his shop. The small living room had candlelight to see by. She couldn't decide if the flickering shadows looked romantic or eerie. Or both.

She looked around at the room. There were bookcases stuffed with books. There was a large poster that showed a chart of the constellations. There was a map of early Salem. There were pots of plants at the windows. This all seemed pretty normal. Sex maniacs probably didn't have places that looked this normal.

She sniffed. Sex maniacs probably didn't have houses that smelled like something delicious was baking. Somehow soothed, Janna sat down on a very old couch. Suddenly, a small black kitten leaped into her lap. It batted at her hair with one paw. Unwillingly charmed, Janna laughed.

"That's Hecate," Ted told her. "Someone left her on my doorstep last month. After some food and a few visits to the vet, she's feeling much happier nowadays."

He rescued cats. He must be a nice guy, right? He might have saved a black cat named Hecate, of course, and he might call himself a witch, but he had done a nice thing.

"Let me fix you some tea." He moved to the small kitchenette in the corner. "I guarantee you'll feel better after some."

She watched, dreamily, as he put a kettle on the small, old-fashioned stove. He took a tin down from an open cupboard. The man was a neat freak. He had no doors on those kitchen cupboards and everything looked incredibly tidy on the shelves.

She watched him mix something in the teacup as he poured the hot water. When he brought it to her, she sniffed it. "This isn't tea." What was he doing to her drink? The man might be gorgeous but she wasn't a complete idiot.

"Chamomile," he answered.

"What's that?" Janna had a dim memory of her grandmother talking about chamomile. If Grandma took it, how bad could it be? Still—

His dimple came and went.

"It'll calm you down. I can tell you're tense." He could tell she wasn't reassured.

"It's just a plant. You can use it for medicinal purposes," he told her. "I'll drink some first if you want, Janna."

He wasn't going to make her feel stupid. She held out the cup and he held her hand as he sipped.

She took both the cup and her hand back, suddenly realizing how intimate it felt to sip from the same cup. Everything he did felt a little too intimate right now. Or not intimate enough. Janna sipped anyhow.

She had to remember he'd expected someone else when he kissed her senseless. Someone he must know pretty well. She had to remember this was business.

Ted smiled at her as she sipped and Janna could feel her body go on instant alert. That smile was so charming. She wasn't feeling like this was business at all.

"How long have you lived in Salem?" he asked her.

"Forever. I went to college and all but then I came back. I have no reason to be so attached to the place but I must be. I'm even willing to commute to work as long as I can live here." She could small talk with the best of them. "How about you?"

"Oh, I moved here recently."

"Why? Oh, yeah. You're a witch. Witches probably love Salem." Janna put her teacup down and shrugged. "Though that makes no sense at all. People were killed here for being witches. Even worse, they weren't witches at all. That's Salem's big claim to fame and it's just stupid."

Ted frowned but his voice remained calm. "When you sell books on mysticism and Magick, then being located in Salem makes sense. It's good publicity. And I'm afraid I need to argue with you about a few things. Intolerance isn't stupid and that was what the Witch Trials are known for. I'm not strictly speaking, a witch, though I do practice Wicca when it seems right. And some of the people involved in the trial may well have been witches." Ted held up fingers of his hand and ticked off the points, one for each finger, as he spoke.

Janna could feel her adrenaline kick in as she sat up. "If you read the transcripts of those trials and, believe me, if you've lived in Salem all your life you have to read them at least once, you'd know not one accused person there was a witch. Even the ones who confessed were obviously crazy." She kind of liked arguing with this guy, even if she had no interest in the subject.

"I didn't say they were the witches." A timer dinged suddenly and Ted got up. "I have some just-baked cinnamon buns. Care for any?"

Well, she'd like a certain kind of buns but that didn't look like anything she'd get tonight. Janna nodded, just to get a good look at those other buns that walked over to get the food out of the oven.

"It's hot." He broke off a small piece and, juggling it, brought it to her. "Try some first."

She blew on the piece.

"What do you mean? Who were the witches?" She took a bite of a delicious sticky bun.

"Their judges."

Janna swallowed the bun down a little too quickly and began to choke. "Where did you get that idea from, Ted?"

"My family history. I have a respected ancestor who was part of the trial and who passed his witchcraft down through the generations. He went along with everyone else in town for fear he might be found out himself." Ted handed her a napkin. "We never talked about it much in our family. But when I moved here I felt like I ought to make amends. I'm just not sure how."

Such a nice body and such a weak mind. Janna could cry over the waste. She wanted to open her mouth and blast him. Or be businesslike. Instead she said, in a dreamy voice that was unlike her own, "You are so gorgeous."

Janna blushed. She hadn't done that in a long time. Why in heaven's name had she suddenly decided to blurt that out, even if it was the truth? And what was the man going to say after that? This was going to be embarrassing.

Ted held himself completely still, his eyes not moving from hers. Janna could feel her heart suddenly start beating faster, then faster yet. Now she wasn't embarrassed. She was horny and expectant. How had the mood between changed so quickly from an almost argument to breathless waiting?

Then Janna realized maybe the mood had never changed at all. She'd been waiting to say those words to him ever since she'd been kissed. His smile suddenly flashed at her, charming, warming, seducing. He moved next to her on the couch and very deliberately put his arm around her shoulders.

"Cinnamon is an aphrodisiac. Did you know that? And is it working as claimed?" His lips were very close to hers.

"I didn't know. But I see you did. I appreciate the effort, but I don't think you needed to do anything extra for me." Janna knew she shouldn't be saying those things but, once again, she couldn't stop herself. "I've been hot for your body ever since I got to have it all over me at the door. Have we talked enough now? I'm easy. Can I have your body all over me again?"

He didn't answer in words. Then again, they really had talked enough. He moved right into action. Ted didn't bother to take her dress off. He bent and sucked on her breast through the fabric. Her nipple immediately came to attention and she could feel the sexual tug along with the physical one as he went to work with his tongue and teeth.

She bit back a cry. One of his hands quickly went under her dress and slid immediately past her panties to begin fondling some very wet parts of her body. Janna almost leapt off the couch at his touch.

If it had been Paul, she would have slapped him for jumping the gun at their first meeting. But this was Ted. She felt like she'd already waited far too long for him to bite her just there, to press his finger on her clit just so.

Instead of slapping, Janna spread her legs wider, hoping for still more.

Ted wasn't slow to respond to the invitation. He pulled her dress up. Then he leaned back, moved to kneel between her legs and she watched his lips blow out in a slow, almost soundless, whistle of admiration. She liked seeing the heat in those blue eyes, but she wanted more.

"Put your hands back on me, you tease." Janna knew the words came out sexy and suggestive, but the two of them both knew it was also an order.

"Maybe. I need to do a few other things first." He winked at her and then quickly pulled that long black T-shirt of a dress over her head. He paused again to study her.

His eyes looked everywhere, a small smile still on his face. Janna hoped he wasn't noticing the extra pounds she'd put on from working late nights instead of working out, or the small scar she had on her knee from a long-ago bicycle accident, or…

"Oh yes. I like this," he whispered. "I like every last inch of your body, Miss O'Neill. And I'm going to like exploring that body of yours tonight, too."

"Don't I get to explore too?" she asked.

She was clenching her teeth to keep from sitting up and grabbing at whatever she could find to suck at or fondle. Janna knew she'd never felt like this before. Maybe it was because she'd been so long without anyone; maybe it was because he was so good-looking; maybe…

Naw. Charms and aphrodisiacs didn't work. Did they?

But it's a special time. Samhain. Time for the Wheel to begin again. Time to celebrate the dead.

"Ted, you aren't…you haven't…" Janna didn't even know what to ask. She didn't know where she was getting these thoughts. What was Samhain anyhow? Probably she was so tired she had no ability to think clearly tonight.

Besides she couldn't think clearly while Ted was taking off his clothes. He looked good in his black T-shirt and jeans, but he looked even better as he got rid of them. Once they were off, Janna couldn't help it. She reached out to touch the hair on his chest, flexing her fingernails into that chest almost like Hecate might.

She paused when she saw the chain he had around his neck and the amulet on it. A five-pointed star with a circle around it. A pentacle. A pentagram.

"I'm a Wiccan, Janna." Ted bent over so the cold metal rested between her breasts. Then he deliberately trailed his hot tongue to the same spot. "Wiccans use the pentacle to show Earth, Air, Fire, Water, and Spirit. The Magick elements. Don't fear that, Janna."

"But…"

"I don't worship the devil. Is that what you are afraid of, sweetheart?" His mouth fastened on one nipple again. She could feel that lovely, long cock close, very close to entering her.

"No. I don't fear anything." Janna could barely say the words.

"I think you're fibbing, sweetheart. But it's not Satan-worship you dislike. Or not entirely. You don't want to know anything about the Old Ways." He was so maddeningly close! Why did he have to keep talking?

"That's not fear or dislike. That's…sensible. Damn it, Ted, are you going to go ahead and fuck me or not?" She could see them locked together in her mind's eye. She could feel that cock moving inside her. But that was all her imagination. He was still poised, almost but not quite where she needed him to be.

Where he had to be. *This minute.*

Just as she realized she would fall apart without more, he thrust—hard and urgent and deep—inside her. She heard the near-scream she gave before she lifted her legs up and over his shoulders. Even this wasn't enough. She wanted more of him.

Locked together, the two of them stared into each other's eyes. The sound of their breathing filled the room. She could only imagine how wild her eyes looked by seeing the ferocity in his. He wasn't charming right now. Ted was powerful and frightening and quite overwhelming. But she wasn't afraid. She wanted to be overwhelmed.

"You're being very difficult, love." He spoke as if he could barely piece the words into a sentence. Maybe he was the one overwhelmed.

"You too." Her voice sounded as breathless and hoarse as his. She didn't know if she wanted words now. She wanted—

He gave a quick laugh that died away into a groan deep in his throat. Then he buried his face between her breasts once again and began to move. That was what she wanted. Hot. So hot. And hard and slick and wet. Exactly what she wanted. Janna shut her eyes to concentrate on just how good he felt inside her.

What she was experiencing was almost too much. She could almost feel sparks of electricity jolting through her. She felt weightless, dizzy, floating.

Having Ted hard and eager between her thighs was erotic, yes, damned erotic, but also more. She didn't know, couldn't figure out what that more was though, when she was so close to a familiar shattering. She felt like the sea was swirling inside her, like the tide pulling away and then smashing back. Soon it would sweep over her completely. Oh God, she wanted it to wash her away. She wanted…

His skilled hand reached out to stroke her clit, gently at first, then more demandingly as he surged inside her again and again. He stiffened as she arched upward. The wail started off thin and desperate and gained in intensity. Finally, finally, finally. Almost. Oh, please. Almost.

Now!

She wasn't sure if the cry was her voice or his, or resonating inside of her head. He groaned as he shuddered within her, one last desperate thrust… It rose as he too shattered, then fell exhausted at her side.

They held each other for a long time afterwards. Janna wasn't sure what to say even if she had the desire or energy to say it. It felt so comfortable to be there with Ted. Comfortable and exciting both.

Had she thought her climax was going to be a familiar sensation? She'd been wrong. This orgasm had been the most amazing one she could remember. Her body was still going through aftershocks. Besides, Ted was still deep inside her, though he must be completely depleted. He still felt right, resting inside her.

Finally she felt the very last of his erection slipping away and out of her. Janna sighed. Ted made a quiet sound, almost in protest, and then propped her body up against his chest as he made to rise.

"Well then, my Janna-Janis O'Neill, are you feeling a little less feisty?" He kissed her under her ear.

"I don't like the name Janis." Janna found it hard to work herself into an argumentative mood, but she gave the effort a good try. Could she help it if she was secretly thrilled when he picked her up and carried her into his bedroom? Maybe the room wasn't all that romantic but when he tossed her into the bed she realized it was large and comfortable and just right for any activities two people might want to try out. Ted climbed in after her and propped himself up to look at her.

"That was the name your mother gave you." Ted hadn't lost track of the conversation either, while he stretched out one long strand of red hair. "So pretty. The hair and the name."

"How did you know?"

"Some call red the devil's color, you know." Ted twirled a strand around his wrist.

"Some say a lot of ignorant, stupid things," Janna snapped. "Probably the same people who also say redheads have bad tempers. I'd watch out if I were you."

"I see I'll have to work really hard to get all the attitude out of you." Ted suddenly shifted and put her on top of him. "Then again, I'm getting really turned on by your attitude."

No other man had ever been turned on by her attitude, but Ted couldn't be lying. He was getting hard again. Janna shifted against him, trying not to feel him up too obviously. Then again, why not? She could already feel the lightening starting to threaten between them. She needed to have him again.

"How did you know my childhood name?" Janna managed to get out before the thought slipped away entirely.

"I know everything about you, sweetheart."

Just as he said that, real thunder rolled up and a crack of lightening hit. Janna jumped. Suddenly it began to rain as if every bit of moisture in the clouds was determined to drop all at once. Rain began to pelt hard against the windows. The wind blew hard through the half-opened window.

The lights went out entirely. Even the candles blew out after the last gust of wind.

"Are you all right, sweetheart?" Ted asked, his voice reassuringly near her. Then his hands were on her, which was both reassuring and thrilling.

"Yes, I'm fine. For God's sake, don't stop whatever you had planned on doing!"

Once Janna said that, she heard another condom wrapper open. Then she felt him slide into her again, this time his cock easily finding its way home.

She began tightening around him again even while she fought to remember what they'd been saying. Her brain didn't work at its analytical best though, when a man was reaching up to play with her breasts and beginning to thrust up harder against her. She squeezed as she found her own rhythm.

In the dark everything seemed more intense, more intimate. She felt freer to do just exactly what she wanted to this lovely, unfamiliar male body. Ted was her own personal sex toy for the night. A remarkably responsive, strong sex toy.

But…how could he know her name? Know everything about her? She'd only heard of him a few hours ago.

Janna didn't know anything about him really. What she did know shouldn't be reassuring. He was a Wiccan and proud of it, he had some nutty theory about the Salem witch trials and…oh, yes…he had the biggest, strongest cock she had felt since forever.

Once again her thoughts scattered as she slid herself against him. She couldn't think right now. Later. Once she got this terrible craving for him satisfied.

"Such a sweet, welcoming pussy," he murmured in her ear. "I've been waiting for that welcome for far too long. Much too long."

"I want it hard and fast, Ted." Janna knew her voice had come out desperate and needy, but she couldn't help it. He was resisting her efforts to pick up the pace. "Hurry."

"We'll see. You haven't really experienced me slow and hard yet."

She hadn't? Janna licked her lips at the thought. What a delightful sex toy. As if he knew what she was thinking and didn't like it, Ted abruptly moved away from her. She let out a cry of protest.

Then he pushed her over onto her stomach. Janna tensed. Wait a minute. Just how kinky was this guy?

When he slid into her wet pussy from behind, she gasped. Not too kinky. Just right. Even though she couldn't control what was happening this way, once again Ted seemed to know what she wanted. Then again, he felt so big and she felt so stretched almost any movement he made was almost too much—and just right.

"You like being fucked this way by me?" he whispered in her ear. "Because I love it. I love feeling that tight pussy of yours. I love feeling your round ass."

"Yes. But I love any way you fuck me," Janna gulped.

"That's because my cock was made for your pussy. I knew it the minute I saw you. Before I saw you—" Then, as if he couldn't bear to wait anymore, he shoved hard inside of her.

Slow and hard would have to wait until later. Ted did just what she'd asked for. Hard, fast, harder, faster. Janna bit her lip to try to stop moaning, vaguely embarrassed at how much noise she was making.

Ted made sure she couldn't stay quiet for long. He bent over her and began to nibble on her earlobe. "Your pussy is wet for me, isn't it?"

She didn't want to respond. She grasped at the sheets, trying to maintain control.

"Getting tighter and wetter while I fuck you."

"Yes!" she cried, the word torn from her lips. She felt as if she was on fire. Maybe she was. Everything he did light a flame inside her.

"Come for me, Janna. Come for me. I want to see you come like you've never come for anyone else. Just me." He panted obscene words in her ear, all the while pumping into her. She hadn't known how erotic that could be.

"You want my cock. Tell me how much."

She shut her eyes, fighting the lure of his words.

"Tell me how much you want me," he commanded. He dragged her to the side of the bed so he could stand up and thrust harder. She'd given up any hope of silence.

"I want you…" She gave in. "I want you!"

Janna wasn't sure how often she'd come, but she knew her arms were shaking by the time she felt him shove his cock into her for the last time. His groan was as loud as hers had ever been. It took him forever to finish. God, it was as if he'd never come before.

She sank, head first, onto the bed. Vaguely she heard and felt Ted slide to the floor. Then Janna could feel herself falling into sleep or blacking out, she wasn't sure which.

* * * * *

He toyed with her hair again, his eyes drooping. He should sleep. But he wanted to look at her. Fiery hair, fiery temper, fiery sex. Everything he'd wanted from her.

She sighed a little. Ted half-smiled. She was sweet, too, though she'd probably slap him if he told her that. But he knew. All the things he thought he'd sensed in her were there.

Sweet, sexy, passionate.

And innocent. She still didn't know about the two of them. She'd been willing to join with him even without knowing. Why? He hoped he knew why but he couldn't be sure. Not yet.

He hoped she had sweet dreams. His gut told him she didn't have them often. Tonight he wanted her to think of him and be happy. He wanted everything she thought and breathed and saw to bind her to him. He had counted on that. What he hadn't counted on was how everything that happened was binding him closer to her. Dangerous. She was more dangerous than she looked.

Ted kept watch over his prize until he, too, finally succumbed to sleep. His arm stretched out, even as his eyes finally shut, and he held onto her tightly.

*****

I am innocent! I am innocent! Innocent!

Janna woke up feeling totally disoriented and panicked again. She opened her eyes and stared blankly up at the ceiling. Where was she?

An arm draped over her chest gave her the first clue. That arm was attached to a hand that cupped her breast when she stirred and then dropped back down again limply.

That felt pleasant but who…Treadwell. She was sleeping with Treadwell. Janna blinked. She was awake now, despite her latest bad dream, and her brain was functioning more sanely.

Why had she decided to sleep with Ted Grimes? Janna took a quick peek at the muscled body next to hers. The face was hidden by his dark hair, but she had the feeling it was going to look just as good or better than it had last night by candlelight. All right, maybe she knew why she'd decided to sleep with him.

Janna scowled. That was still reckless, irresponsible behavior. She didn't do things like that.

Then she grinned. Until now, anyhow. So far things had worked out beautifully. She hadn't felt this good in a long time. Not even since she'd last had sex. Janna decided what she needed was a good stretch and a little quiet gloating. Carefully she slid herself out from under Ted's hand and stood up.

Ouch. She had some bruises and twinges. Janna thought about how she'd gotten those bruises and twinges and grinned again.

She peered outside. There was nothing left to show from last night's storm. The streets of Salem looked as cold and autumnal as ever. Janna wondered if that meant the electricity was back on in Ted's upstairs rooms. She moved to a small floor lamp and turned the switch on. Light flowed out.

Janna debated trying to fix herself breakfast. Cooking was not her strong point and she didn't like eating anything she concocted unless she was starving. She decided she wasn't that hungry and that Ted was such a neat freak that he might not want her in his tiny kitchen area. Neatness while cooking was another thing she didn't do well.

Restless, she went to one of his many bookshelves to stare at what he kept for reading material. Most of it seemed to be on herbs or astronomy. Janna yawned. She wasn't interested.

Part of her wanted to go back and pounce on her host again. She knew she was interested in doing that. But part of her warned that she had been pouncing on a stranger too often already.

A book title caught her eye and she snorted. *The Book of Spells* indeed. Did Ted really believe in all this gobbledygook? Rolling her eyes, Janna pulled the book out. If she wasn't going to pounce she might as well read something. As she turned the pages she began to frown again.

--Adder's Mouth, when spread on the offender's doorway, can be used to quiet a gossip.

--Anise is said to increase psychic abilities when taken as a tea.

Janna flipped through the pages impatiently. Then she paused and reread a passage.

To make your man more passionate in bed, write his name on a red phallus-shaped candle.

Candle…Janna looked up and stared at the red candle that still sat on the kitchen counter.

No. Ted hadn't. He couldn't have meant that. Then she thought back.

"Cinnamon is an aphrodisiac. Did you know that?"

Red candles for passion. Cinnamon as an aphrodisiac. Janna swallowed hard. Ted had planned a seduction out? A seduction for her? Things were looking that way. After all, she didn't believe in all this, but Ted obviously did.

But that made no sense. He hadn't been waiting for her. Janna was lucky that whoever it was he had expected when he gave her that first amazing hello hadn't shown up in the middle of their evening. Ted had meant all this for that woman. He didn't even know what she looked like before she'd arrived.

"I know everything about you, sweetheart."

Oh God. That made no sense, either. Had she gotten involved with some kind of Wiccan stalker? Maybe they needed female sacrifices. Janna smothered a nervous giggle. If they needed virgin female sacrifices then Ted had obviously messed up.

Another thought hit her. When did they have a rainstorm in late October or early November? Snow, yes. But rain? It was cold out there. Janna ran to the window and looked out again just to be sure. No trace of rain, ice, or snow.

Oh no. And those weird thoughts she'd been getting — no, please let them be from jetlag or overwork. Ted couldn't do that to her, could he?

"I don't like this," Janna whispered to herself.

She turned and began to look for her clothing. The bra was draped over the couch. Her dress was in a tiny ball on the floor. One shoe was near the door and Hecate was curled up near the other. Some shredded black pantyhose lay nearby.

Janna couldn't find her panties. As she struggled into her dress, she decided she didn't need them. Let Ted keep them for a memento. God knows what he'd do with them. Weirdo.

She glanced his way. All right. He was a well-hung, well-built weirdo. But she didn't need to get anymore involved than she already was. Halloween was over. She'd had her trick *and* treat.

Now what she needed to do was get out. Janna eyed her shoes thoughtfully. It was cold and those heels weren't made for walking. She shoved them on her feet.

How would she get home? Her friends wouldn't be around. Erica didn't even live nearby. Anyhow, Nancy and Erica were probably out with their normal new guys having a normal morning-after experience. Fine. She wouldn't call them. There had to be a diner or coffee shop somewhere nearby. Her purse was tipped over behind the kitchen counter. Janna grabbed it. She could call a cab from the next pay phone she saw.

She hoped Ted didn't have a modern security system with alarms that would go off when she opened the door. Because she planned to open that door right now —

No sound. No alarm. Janna breathed out and began to ease down the stairs. She was halfway down when she heard a sleepy, "Janna?"

She began to take the steps two at a time.

"Janna!" His voice was definitely no longer sleepy.

The door was deadbolt locked but the key hung on a hook next to the door. After all, Ted was a tidy kind of guy. Janna pushed the key in, turned it and heard loud noises upstairs.

"Where the hell are you, Janna?"

She pulled the door open and ran out into the early November morning.

* * * * *

Where the hell was a place to get in from the cold and make a phone call when you needed one? Janna cursed the small purse that had made her decide not to take her cell phone with her. She cursed the high-heeled shoes she had decided made her look sexy. She cursed the cold climate of Salem. She was going to get around to cursing witches who seduced her as soon as she had the energy to think up something really nasty.

When she finally saw the tiny all-night diner she could have cried with relief. She'd get a cab and she'd get home. Janna thought of her tiny little apartment. She hadn't been home in weeks. Right now she craved being there. She'd get to take a hot bath and root around for some comfortable pajamas. Too bad it was too early to call for a pizza. She could eat a whole pizza deluxe special herself right now. Since there was practically no food in her place she'd knew she'd have to make do with some dry Fruit Loops cereal instead. She thought about cursing that later, too.

As she put her hand on the door to the restaurant, another hand covered hers. She stared at the large, strong fingers and didn't even have to look up to know who was there.

"What happened, Janna? Why did you run away?"

He sounded angry. Angry and worried. But mostly angry.

"I'm going inside, I'm calling a taxi, and if you try to stop me I'm going to scream until someone calls the police." Janna made her voice sound firm.

"I wouldn't dream of stopping you." Ted opened the door with a flourish.

Janna stepped inside. Oh, yes. The diner was warm and she could smell coffee. That was as close to heaven as she needed this morning.

There was also a payphone by the entrance. She could call that taxi. Ted's hand on the small of her back steered her into a back booth instead. Janna thought about telling him no and then sniffed the coffee aroma again. She could stay for a cup of coffee.

The waitress who came to their booth looked tired.

"What's your pleasure?" she asked.

"Coffee. Black." Janna said.

"Do you have any herbal teas?" Ted asked.

The waitress looked confused. "Decaf?"

"Close enough. And get the lady and myself some scrambled eggs with toast." Ted relaxed back into the booth, his eyes still on Janna.

"Why do you assume I'll eat scrambled eggs and toast?" Janna loved scrambled eggs and toast and was starving, but that wasn't the point.

"We depleted a lot of energy last night. I'm sure you're hungry." Ted tapped his finger on the table. "And I certainly don't want you to get sick."

"Listen, Treadwell." Janna tried to sound as snide as she could. She knew she could usually do a fine job without trying. "I don't know what sort of mind game you're playing here, but I'm opting out."

"You can't, Janna. You're too perfect."

She loved how his blue eyes glinted when he smiled. God, he was an attractive man.

No. No, she wasn't going to let her mind wander again. The last time she did that, they'd ended up hot and sweaty and all over each other. She had to remember that was a bad thing.

"Perfect for what?" She had to remember he was also doing something strange, something she couldn't quite figure out yet.

"Well, for me." He didn't even look sheepish when he said that.

Janna just stared at him. Ted took both her hands. "Sweetheart, I've been looking for you for years. Ever since I realized my family history."

"Why?" Janna wasn't even sure she wanted to know. "And—and you didn't expect me to be there last night when you pounced on me."

"I lied about that. Well, sort of." He spoke faster when he saw her reaction to his words. "I did expect Janis-Janna O'Neill. I knew you had lived in Salem forever, you were going to make a sales pitch to me, and a million and one other things. But I'd never met you. When you showed up, I just gave in to an impulse that got a little out of hand. But you were so responsive. So perfect."

"I was sex-starved, you mean?"

"No! I mean, I knew I'd been right. You were the one I needed."

"For what, damn it?"

"To make amends."

Janna wondered if anyone would be upset if she dumped some coffee in the lap of the exasperating creature in front of her. Once she explained, surely people would sympathize with her.

"For *what*?" Janna kept her voice down, but just barely. She saw the waitress glance her way.

"I told you last night."

"Oh, remind me." Janna managed the words through her gritted teeth. She wanted to scream but reminded herself he might have explained something in his own convoluted Wiccan fashion. He probably even thought she understood. She'd wait to scream until after he explained. "Perhaps it slipped my mind."

"My ancestors hung one of yours, knowing full well that she wasn't a witch and he was." Ted looked at her as if what he said should make complete sense.

"My last name is O'Neill. My great-great grandparents came over from the Old Country long after the witch trials." Janna resisted patting Ted on the shoulder.

"That was only one branch of your family, sweetheart. Tell the truth. Haven't you felt…uneasy, sometimes? I can tell things about people, you know. Not always clearly, but I know you've been troubled by something that took place in the past." Ted looked up as the waitress came over with their food. He smiled at her as he thanked her and she beamed.

The man was a charmer, no doubt about it. Out of his mind, but a charmer.

"No. I haven't. The past has never troubled me much. I live in the present." Janna forked a mouthful of scrambled eggs.

"You haven't had anything bother you? Dreams perhaps?"

Janna paused in chewing. She forced herself to swallow the eggs rather than choke. The old woman. The voices in her dreams. How did he know? Oh Lord, he didn't really know everything about her, did he?

"Dreams can bother me sometimes. They can bother anyone." Janna tried to make it casual.

"But—"

"Listen, you set me up. From the time you talked to my agency to when you first kissed me like you were going to ravish me—"

"I did ravish you, Janna."

"—to setting up those damned superstitious candles and cinnamon buns. And all to atone for something your ancestors did? That's weird!" Janna pushed her plate away. "I'm calling a cab."

"I'll take you home, Janna. Soon. Let me finish. It's not just to atone. Or, rather, it's not just because I feel guilty. My family has had problems ever since my ancestor the judge helped condemn yours to death." Ted pinched the bridge of his nose with his fingers. "Sort of—well, a curse."

Janna dropped her head in her hands and moaned. She did *not* need this. First Paul the loser and now Ted the lunatic. Was there something wrong with her? How did she attract these guys?

"What kind of curse?" Janna said, bracing herself. "You die at age thirty. You howl at the moon at midnight. You all grow up to be raving insane sex maniacs?"

"Shhhh." Ted replied. The other diners had looked up again. "Nothing like that. We…we just have a hard time falling in love."

"Huh?"

"Your ancestor, Dorcas, told the judge that since he had no pity, his family would find no love. She wasn't a witch, but she had right on her side. What she said came true for my family."

"I don't remember that in any of the Salem records," Janna objected.

"So you remember what you read of the trial transcripts!" Ted had an annoying grin on his face. "You must have had some interest in the trials."

"It's drilled into you in school," Janna scoffed.

She shut her eyes. She did remember the words, or some of them. She ought to be able to remember. She'd finally made the connection, although it had taken her long enough. Those words had been echoing in her dreams for weeks. *Innocent. I am innocent.*

"She didn't say it where others could record the words. Janna, I know how this sounds to you. I feel stupid enough telling you and I'm more used to all this than you. But try to understand. All our lives my family has been…cold. Unable to connect to people. You wouldn't believe the number of unhappy marriages and divorces we've had over the generations. I decided to study why and I told myself I was never going to try to get close to anyone if I couldn't change things." Ted put his hand on her knee.

Janna glared, but that hand felt sort of nice there. Fine. She was weak. She let the hand stay.

"I studied the family history. I began to look up your ancestor's family tree. I know your cousins, your sisters, your brother."

"Several of my cousins are single. Why not try charming them?"

"I wanted you. Something about…well, when I saw your name I just knew you were the right one. At least I hoped so." Why did he have to look so sincere? "Something about just your name appealed to me."

"Janis?"

"Yeah. Janis. Janna is fine, too. But I met you on paper as Janis Katherine Dorcas O'Neill."

Janna tried not to squirm. "You really do know everything about me. Even the Dorcas."

"I know a lot. I'd love to know more."

"Ted, you don't really. You used me. You set me up and used me to get rid of some imaginary family curse of yours." Janna tried not to let the idea depress her as much as it seemed to be doing. "Let's finish all this. I don't have a lot of cash with me. We can stop at an ATM on the way to my house and I'll pay you my share of breakfast. Then we can just say good-bye."

Ted didn't say anything, though he didn't look happy. They both stood up and, while Ted paid the bill at the counter, Janna contemplated how stupid she'd been last night.

She had to get in touch with Nancy or Erica. They'd help sort out all the messy emotions she was feeling. Everything hurt. Janna gritted her teeth. She just needed to endure a few more minutes with Ted and then she would never have to endure him again.

Damn it, that idea hurt too.

Ted didn't stop at an ATM on the way back. Janna was suddenly feeling too depressed to even try to fight about why he didn't. She stared out the window, looking at the bleak grayness of the morning. It was going to be one of those dark, chilling days. Perfect. That was just the way she felt.

When they got to her place, Ted parked the car. Janna let out a sigh.

"Well, thanks," she managed.

Ted opened the door for her and said, "I'm seeing you to the door, like it or not."

Janna didn't look at him as they went past the lobby. Still, it seemed to take forever before she got to her door. Janna put her key in, opened the door, flicked on the hall light and then turned to him.

"Well, good-bye then."

"I don't think so."

Ted didn't sound charming at all. Janna wondered how many other people had seen the real Ted, the intense, almost spooky one. That side of Ted was hidden under the charm and the good looks but just as much a part of him.

"Listen, you need to understand that this is my place, Mr. Grimes..." Janna began.

He walked into her place behind her and then shut the door with a push of his shoulder. "No. You need to understand something, Ms. O'Neill. Several somethings."

"What?"

"First, those spells and charms were because I was scared, not because I wanted to trick you. I already knew you were important to me and I didn't want you to leave before we'd had the chance to really talk."

"You think we talked last night?" Janna tried to laugh scornfully.

"No. But I'd like to now."

Janna glanced down at Ted's pants and suddenly the confused hurt rolled away. "You need to explain how much you'd like to talk to your cock down there. I don't think he's listening."

Ted's smile was blinding again.

"Well, I wouldn't mind talking and fucking, Janna. They are two of my favorite things to do…especially with you." Then, suddenly, he was holding her again. His hungry mouth moved softly, persuasively, against her lips until she let him inside.

He was persuasive, but definitely not soft. His tongue glided against hers. His hands held her arms as he moved against her, showing just how hard he was.

It was just like the first time. And, once again, this was a bad idea. Probably. On the other hand, that tongue was still very persuasive. Janna knew she shouldn't, but she felt herself relaxing into that body and mouth.

"No charms, no tricks this time, Janna. It's just me, wanting you desperately," Ted's voice rasped in her ear. "Your choice, sweetheart."

Choice? She had no choice. Janna's head swam as she moved her mouth to let her tongue explore his chin and jaw. He had a morning stubble. That should annoy her but didn't. Ted made it exciting to be scratched by his whiskers.

Love is yours. Just look for the truth inside.

For a second she remembered that crazy witch-woman. She wasn't sure love was hers, but she was willing to finally look at the truth — her truth — inside. Was love was hers? She hoped love could be hers. Lord, she hoped so.

"I want you too. No. More than that. You're becoming important to me, Ted," Janna admitted. "This is nuts and we're probably going to kill each other before the week is out, though. You and I are so different."

"I like where we're different." Ted's hand explored some of the difference under her dress. "And if we kill each other before the week is over, it'll be from too much sex. I've always thought that was a great way to go. Especially with someone you're starting to love. I don't really know how love works, Janna, but I have a feeling I may find out with you. Why else did something tell me you were the person I needed to search for?"

He was always going to think in ways that defied logic. Janna already knew that. But how could she argue when they were both coming to the same conclusion? Besides, she really did want to stop talking and make use of that cock. Immediately.

"All right then," Janna said, thickly, unsnapping his jeans. "Don't say I didn't warn you."

At that, without warning, the lights went out.

Ted laughed and ripped her dress off. Janna didn't know which action to be more stunned by. At least things weren't as dark as last night. She could see Ted in the murky morning light, his mouth now fastened on one of her nipples.

"You told me no tricks!" Janna almost wailed, but she wasn't sure she was wailing over his deceit or the way his teeth felt on her nipple. "You turned the damn lights off again!"

Ted looked up. "That wasn't me, Janna. That's you. Or perhaps it's you and me together. We're a powerful combination, darling." Then he went back to what he'd been doing.

"I can't—Damn it, Ted, don't do that—oooh, that does feel good. Touch me there again. No, wait. Ted, I have nothing to do with electricity—yes, there—I mean, I didn't make the lights go out."

Janna knew she wasn't exactly making sense, but how could she think when his hands were stroking her clit so knowingly and his mouth was nipping and licking her second nipple into a long, hard point?

"Oh yes, you do." Ted sounded as if he was struggling to concentrate. "That's when I was sure we were meant for each other. You blow my house's fuses as well as mine. Oh, God, Janna! Do that again."

Janna had finally discovered the pleasure of trying to talk and fuck at the same time. And torturing your partner with sex while you listened to what he was saying. Janna bit the tip of her tongue hard as she used her hands to grasp Ted's delightful penis.

"You're saying this is my fault?" Janna asked.

"Right now everything is your fault, sweetheart," Ted groaned. "Including the light failure."

He picked her up and almost threw her on the floor.

"Damn, Ted, I'm going to get carpet burns!" Janna yelped.

"Serves you right." Ted nipped her thigh and she yelped again.

And then it was much too late to laugh or joke or do anything but let the increasing passion and tension build. Janna whimpered as her legs clung to Ted's waist. She'd been the crazy one to think she wanted to be rid of him or of this forever.

"Did you really think you could give up the feel of my cock inside you? Or that I'd leave that warm pussy of yours?" Ted grinned at her as he slid his cock deeper into her aching sheath, grinding his hips against her. "Tell me what you want."

"You!" Janna didn't care how desperate she sounded anymore. She didn't care about anything but the feel of his cock sliding inside her.

She drummed at his back with her heels, demanding more. She knew she scratched and cried and squeezed trying to get more. Ted understood her perfectly and gave her what she demanded, sinking his hard, hot cock into her over and over again. The sound of their bodies slamming together became a music of its own, like the roar of the waves at the sea. She thought she might go through the floor with some of his thrusts.

Janna knew she couldn't stand more. "Now!" she screamed. Lightning seemed to crack in the air. Suddenly the tension released into one overwhelming surge of bliss. As she cried out her climax, the light went back on above her. Ted groaned a half-second later, shuddering over her. Janna shut her eyes again, just enjoying the feel of his body quaking against hers.

"Now whose fault is it?" Ted demanded at last in a faint voice. "It wasn't my climax that made the lights go back on, Ms. O'Neill!"

Ted was getting much too good at arguing.

"Never mind that," Janna sidestepped. "What kind of amends did you have in mind, Ted?"

"What?"

"You said you needed to make amends to my family or me." Janna pushed her hair back and got up on her elbows to survey her somewhat worse-for-wear lover. "What did you have in mind?"

Ted smiled. "If you think I haven't done enough, I guess I'll just have to atone some more." He reached for her again.

Janna laughed and squirmed. "I don't think I meant that, exactly," she protested.

"I did...I really do want to try for some slow and hard—and tender—sex with you. Shall we try again now? You're much too charming to keep my hands off you for long."

Damn. Wait until she told Erica and Nancy that someone had actually called her charming. Janna's fingers curled themselves into Ted's long hair. Then again, she could wait to tell them. She had more important things to do. Like charm the man again.

About the author:

Treva Harte read far too many romances for far too long. One day the inevitable happened. She started writing her own brand of romance. She claims taking care of the family's neurotic miniature dachshund and raising two elementary school age kids is a full time job in itself, but she also works full time as an attorney in a city with many other attorneys. She and her husband both like writing in whatever time they have left, so they often fight over -- whoops, since they are attorneys they NEGOTIATE over -- keyboard time.

Treva Hart welcomes mail from readers. You can write to them c/o Ellora's Cave Publishing at P.O. Box 787, Hudson, Ohio 44236-0787.

Also by Treva Harte:

- His Mistress
- Intimate Choices
- Naughty or Nice
- No Time To Dream
- Perfect
- The Deviants
    - The Deviants
    - Changing The Odds
    - World Enough
- The Seduction of Sean Nolan
- The Wildling
- Things That Go Bump In The Night
- Threshold Volume 1
- Twisted Destiny
- Why Me
- Wicked

Naughty Nancy
Book 4 ½: Trek Mi Q'an Part II

By Jaid Black

To Dot's margaritas & Lori's scenarios
To Crissy & knowledge-seeking
To Kris & love grottos <g>
To Maryam & patience [ahem]
To Mary & cheap husbands *sigh*
To Marty & cheap husbands *another sigh*
To Gis & Lamby *very big sigh*
To NN's harem & kadin *wiggles eyebrows*

To the women on the Jaid Black bulletin board…
…for grinning knowingly when you read this.
I'll see you in Scotland, Nancy ;)

Chapter 1

Hunting Grounds of the F'al Vader Pack
Planet Khan-Gor ("Planet of the Predators")
Seventh Dimension, 6067 Y.Y. (Yessat Years)

"*Ahhh…CHOO!*"

Nancy's eyes squinted shut as her entire body shuddered from the violence of a sneeze. She sneezed three times more in rapid succession, then waved her hands madly about to clear the puff of whitish smoke that was swirling around her like a cranky cloud.

Damn it! she mentally wailed. What weird concoction had that old witch blown at her? It was translucent white and very sticky, much like a resin.

Nancy harrumphed as she absently studied her hands. She never should have decided to take a break from Lori's party. She never should have exited outside to the back alley in order to regain her composure. So what if a man had engaged her in conversation, she thought acidly. Any *normal* woman would have been able to sustain a casual conversation with a man without finding it necessary to take a break and air herself out before resuming said conversation.

Damn it!

Nancy's lips pinched together in a glower. Perhaps she really should have taken that job in Alaska. She doubted she would have gotten so fidgety around a mountain man. She doubted she would have cared whether or not such a male found her impressive enough to seduce. Her biggest concern with impressing a mountain man would have been whether or not she looked inbred enough to suit his sexual taste.

Nancy's back went ramrod straight. *Damn it!*

This was enough mental babbling, she babbled to herself. She'd gotten her air—as well as some weird sticky white junk blown at her by the feisty old witch!—so it was time to go back inside and continue the conversation she'd been having but minutes prior with Justin. Justin seemed like a good enough sort, she assured herself with a harrumph. He wasn't an athletic hunk by any stretch of the imagination, but then again she doubted Playboy would be contacting her anytime soon begging her to pose for a centerfold spread.

Her lips pinched together in a frown. *Damn it!*

Nancy supposed that if she possessed a body worthy of Playboy, she probably wouldn't be so damned unsure of herself where the opposite gender was concerned. But she didn't and she was. She'd just have to figure out a way to get over it.

One thing was for certain, she thought as she finished clearing the air of the whitish smoke with her hands, her goal of getting laid tonight would be a hell of a lot easier to accomplish if Justin were a more forceful type. As is she felt as if she was the one doing all the seducing—hardly an easy feat for a woman who'd been known as a reclusive social mouse not even a full day ago.

Nancy took a deep breath as she squared her shoulders.

It was time to go back inside. It was time to rejoin the party. It was time to seduce the hell out of nerdy, geeky

Justin. She was a warrior woman now, she reminded herself with a sniff. Xena. Phoenix from the—

Bah! She was going to fuck that little dweeb tonight if it was the last thing she ever did. Enough said.

Her chin went up a notch. Her nostrils flared. She was determined, damn it. Horny and determined. She hadn't purchased those condoms tucked away in her scabbard for nothing.

Gritting her teeth, she took a resolute step toward the backdoor entrance to Lori's party. Warrior woman, she silently reiterated as her nostrils flared impossibly further. Alpha female, she silently grunted, her muscles flexing.

It was time to go back inside. It was time to rejoin the party. It was time to…

It was time to figure out where in the hell she was.

"Oh shit." Nancy's jaw dropped open as the air finally cleared of the whitish smoke and she got her first unimpeded look at her surroundings. Her eyes widened and her teeth clicked shut as it dawned on her that she was standing in some sort of a…nest?

"What the hell," she muttered.

Nancy gaped down at her feet, noting that the structure she was standing in was silver and glittery, the fabric of it similar to that of twined tree bark—silver, glittery, twined tree bark. Worse yet, there were animal pelts scattered all about the nest, as if it had been recently occupied.

She gulped. If the nest had been recently occupied, it didn't take an Einstein to figure out that whatever had occupied it would probably come back. And it might not like to share…

"Shit." Her heart pounding, Nancy swore under her breath as she quickly made her way to the other side of the glittery silver nest. The nest swayed a bit, so she immediately came to a standstill, then crept slowly to the side, careful not to rock it.

She was in shock, she knew. She had no idea where she was or how she had gotten here but—

"Oh. My. God." Nancy's entire body froze in place when she reached one wall of the nest and glanced to the terrain that surrounded it. Or more to the point, when she glanced to the terrain that *didn't* surround it. "I am in a damn tree," she said in a monotone. "The witch actually put me in a tree."

In so much as she could tell, there was no land on any side of the nest to step off onto. It appeared to be high up—very, very high up, she uneasily noted—perched up in a tree and surrounded on all sides by a towering view of a silverish, icy-looking mountainscape hundreds of feet below it.

Her heart rate soared. Silver-ice mountains? Hundreds of feet *below* her?

She gulped. She'd always been afraid of heights. The nest she was currently standing in was up higher than she'd ever been before. If she couldn't see any land directly below the nest, then that could only mean that—

She gasped, noting for the first time that a pointed piece of silver ice jutted up from the middle of the nest. That could only mean that...

She swallowed roughly. That could only mean that...

That could only mean that the nest was impaled upon a narrow, pointed piece of icecap. One singular piece of ice was all that held the nest up, she thought hysterically, was all that stood between keeping the nest perched upright on the mountain apex and allowing the nest to plummet only God knows how far to the ground.

Damn it! I'm going to kill that witch!

Blood rushed to Nancy's head, pounded through her veins. Her heart rate accelerated impossibly higher as a near-maddening hysteria bubbled up inside of her. Her eyes wide with fright, she opened her mouth and did the only thing she could think to do in such a situation.

She screamed. Loudly.

"Help Meeeeeeeeeeeeeeeeeeee!"

She screamed out her platitude three times more, her voice hoarse when at last she stopped. Panting for air, she braved another glance over the ledge, immediately noting that the plummet from up in the nest didn't look anymore welcoming than it had before she'd started wailing like a baby.

"Damn it!" she screeched.

Mountains. For as far as the eye could see there was nothing but mountains. And silver ice. The ice was everywhere, coated everything, and formed slick shields on mountains that were so tall she couldn't see their bottoms.

"What. Is. Going. On," she bit out.

A gust of icy wind hit her in the face, inducing her to realize for the first time just how cold it was up here…wherever up here was. Shivering, she raised her hands and began to briskly rub them up and down her arms, absently working the chill bumps out of her flesh while simultaneously wracking her brain for a way out of her predicament.

She bit her lip. She was up in a nest. The nest was perched on top of one of those pointed mountain apexes she'd just seen below. How would she ever get out of here? And when—and if—she did get out, where to then?

Her nostrils flared to wicked proportions. Alaska. Why the hell hadn't she taken that job in Alaska? "Damn old witch," she mumbled under her breath. "I should never have given her my last stick of gum. I should have…"

She didn't know why, couldn't say what premonition it was that instructed her to shut up and look down, but slowly—ever so slowly—Nancy's eyes trailed down her body until she ascertained that…

Yep, she was butt naked.

Damn it!

Ooooh, she thought angrily, her lips coming together to form a snarl, the witch had gone too far this time. Not only was she stuck in a silvery glitter nest made of twined bark, not only was the nest thousands of feet off the nearest ground, not only was her body covered in a sticky white residue, not only was it colder than she didn't know what up here, but she was also naked. Butt naked.

Her hands fisted into tight balls and fell to her sides. When she got out of this place—and she *would* get out of it—she was going to strangle that old witch and enjoy the depraved activity with every cell of her being. So this is the thanks she was to receive for being kind to that woman, she thought melodramatically. She couldn't believe *this* was her reward for being nice enough to give the old woman the last stick of gum she'd had on her, the very one she'd tucked away in her…

"Scabbard." Nancy let out a breath of relief when she realized she might be naked, but she still had her sword and scabbard with her. She didn't know why that knowledge gave her such comfort, but it did. Perhaps it was because the sword was, at present, the only connection she had to the world she'd been transported from. Perhaps it was because the sword—useless as it no doubt was since she didn't know how to use it—would still offer her minimal protection from any predator that might think to reclaim its nest while she was occupying it. Whatever the reason, it did the trick and helped her to calm down a bit.

"I have to get out of here," she murmured, her brown eyes darting warily back and forth.

Just then another gust of chillingly cold wind slammed into her face, inducing her flesh to goosebump. Her teeth chattering, she sank slowly to her knees and ran her hands over one of the animal pelts lining the nest. It was warm and fuzzy, and very inviting at the moment.

As she looked around she noted that the sun was rapidly fading and that darkness would soon overtake this mountain she was stranded atop. The darkness, she thought nervously, would cause the temperature to plummet even lower.

She spent a threadbare moment considering her options, but realized rather quickly that she didn't have any to consider. There was no getting off this mountaintop without aid. She would have to bide her time and pray that the old witch decided to poof her back to Salem in the morning.

Climbing under the intoxicatingly warm animal pelts, Nancy expelled a deep breath as she fell asleep with her sword laid against her backside. It was there, the still-warm metal reassuringly within reaching distance if she needed it.

Drowsy, confused, angry, but mostly frightened, she allowed herself to succumb to slumber, hoping against hope that she was already asleep and would wake up to find that all of this had been no more than a bad dream.

When her gaze flicked up and she took notice of four crimson full moons tinting the nighttime sky atop the mountain a haunting blood red, she closed her eyes and told herself it simply had to be a dream.

A very horrific, intensely frightening, could-drive-a-woman-to-drink, bad dream.

Damn it!

Chapter 2

Vorik F'al Vader, the eldest of seven sons and heir to his sire Yorin's dominion, landed silently on the ground, careful to make not a sound. He shape-shifted immediately from his winged *kor-tar* form and landed on humanoid feet, his heavily muscled body nigh unto naked, save the kilt wrapped about his waist and the pair of knee-high silver *muu* hide boots he wore.

Slowly, his dark-haired head came up, his acute silver eyes scanning the mountainside for any sign of *yenni* movement. He felt the excitement of the hunt coursing through his veins knowing 'twas at long last time to round up his own pen of pets. Some would be bartered at market, aye, but most he would keep for himself.

What made a *yenni* so valuable was not only the she-beast's insatiable hunger for humanoid male seed, but 'twas also the sheer beauty of her fertile form—the fleshiness of her hips, the milkiness of her pale skin, the way she'd daintily flick her tail about whilst she suckled seed from a Khan-Gori male's cock…

Vorik sighed a bit dreamily, and with much anticipation. He had seen eighteen Yessat years as of this moon-rising so now 'twas his rite of passage into manhood to take as many *yenni* as he desired into his keeping…and into his bedfurs. For years he had fantasized about what it might feel like to have a hoard of females suckle from him, drink from him, feed from him. He would care for them well, he knew, making himself and his cock ever available to see to their appetites.

He was a selfless Barbarian, he told himself with a sniff. No matter how much seed his pets would wish to suckle from him, he'd see to it he provided them with it. Aye, he was forever putting the needs of others before his own. He was forever thinking of the happiness of other creatures before he saw fit to care for himself. He was forever—

Bah! He wished to have his cock suckled til 'twas possible it fell off. Enough said.

Vorik took a deep breath and closed his eyes, drinking crisp cold air into his lungs. He needed to calm himself, he knew, for his man sac was already tight and nigh unto bursting just thinking about the hunting booty that would soon be his. 'Twas cruel indeed the ancient custom that forbade a Khan-Gori male to lose his virginity until he saw eighteen Yessat Years, for it seemed that his cock and man sac had been in desperate need of satiation ever since the moon-rising he'd turned twelve.

Every waking moment for the past six years had been hellish, every hour had passed as an eternity, for the need to thrust into the warm, suctioning flesh of his destined mate had come upon him at hourly intervals, nigh unto driving him insane. Because the males of his species realized they weren't likely to find their Bloodmates until much later in life, 'twas the way of it on Khan-Gor to expend one's seed within the bodies of the dimwitted *yenni* until at which time a Bloodmate was claimed. Even then a Khan-Gori male was expected to keep up the feeding of his pets until they were bartered at market, for 'twould be cruel indeed to allow the beautiful creatures to slowly starve to death.

Vorik harrumphed. He could never be so cruel.

As is ever the way of nature, the system worked out just fine, for female *yenni* could not survive without feeding on seed. And so it came to pass through the perfection of trillions of Yessat years of evolution that the *yenni* provided sticky flesh to thrust into and voracious mouths to be suckled with whilst the Khan-Gori male provided his dimwitted pet with food. 'Twas a perfect system. Or, Vorik mentally qualified as his lips turned down grimly, mayhap it would have been a perfect system had he been allowed to indulge of *yenni* from his twelfth year onward.

By the tit of the she-god, he needed a suckling.

A soft purring sound a mile away snagged Vorik's attention, inducing him to smile slowly. He had heard that very sound many a time emitting from the pen his sire's *yenni* were caged in. The sound always meant one of two things—the *yenni* had either fallen asleep after feeding well, or she was cleaning herself.

His nostrils flared as he breathed in the scent of her. It mattered not that she was a mile off in distance, for the males of his species had the most acute sensory systems of any known creature in the seventh dimension of time and space. He could smell her skin, could smell her pussy, could smell the scent of her arousal…

Fangs exploded into Vorik's mouth as he shape-shifted back into his *kor-tar* form. Faster than an eye can blink, his skin dimmed from its usual golden bronze color to a translucent shade of silver ice. Talons that tore prey apart so easily spiked out from where his toes had been, and wings that spanned twelve feet across protruded from his back as he leapt skyward and took flight.

At last, he thought as his manhood hardened, *oh aye at last*.

He tracked her easily, a skill any Khan-Gori male perfected by childhood. Part and parcel of growing into manhood on his planet was learning to provide food for one's family, and one could not provide food for their pack without a hunter's skill at taking down living, moving prey. This *yenni* would provide him with no food, 'twas true, for 'twould be Vorik who provided her with much nourishment.

Oh aye.

He found the *yenni* cleaning herself near unto an ice-coated stream, her face lowered betwixt her thighs and her tongue darting out to lap at her own pussy. Vorik's nostrils flared as he watched her, her pink tongue meticulously rimming the folds of her flesh, then darting up on a purr to lick at the bud nestled between the lips of flesh. She purred and cooed as she lapped at herself, and Vorik found himself simply staring at the beauty of the scene.

This *yenni* female was nigh unto perfect in her beauty. Her creamy breasts were large, the pink nipples that capped them round and full. Her hair was long and dark, and looked soft to the touch. The only aspect of the she-beast he found to be a turn-off was the thinness of her form. 'Twas obvious she was no alpha female for a dominant she-beast would better know how to feed on male seed.

Well, Vorik grunted, verily it mattered not, for he would teach the she-beast whatever lessons she needed to learn in the art of feeding. 'Twould be ideal if she already knew what she was about, but such was apparently not the way of it. So no matter how many sucklings it took to teach her how to get great spurts of seed in one feeding, he would be patient and understanding in waiting for her to catch on.

By the tit of the she-god, he grumbled as he licked his fangs, he prayed she was as dimwitted as she looked.

Vorik's cock stiffened whilst he landed on his feet and shape-shifted into his humanoid form. His fangs retreated, his wings and talons seemingly disappeared, as he softly made his way through the thick of the trees to stalk and capture the *yenni* by the stream. He was careful to make not a sound as he prowled toward the open savannah from the forest, no cracking of ice under his feet, no rustling of branches overhead.

"Help Meeeeeeeeeeeeeeeeeee!"

Vorik's entire body stilled as the feeding call of an alpha female *yenni* reached his ears. The shrill cry of the dominant female caused the *yenni* he'd been tracking but moments prior to whimper and scamper away, and he found himself uncaring of the fact that he'd just been thwarted of his hunting booty for he was intrigued indeed by this unexpected happening.

Verily, 'twas hard to stalk an alpha female. 'Twas even harder to track one who sounded to be desperately hungry for they tended to stay well-fed. Mayhap, he thought to himself, she had followed a Khan-Gori predator to a hunting perch in the hopes of getting a meal and had managed to snare herself into a nest from which she could not escape in the doing.

"Help Meeeeeeeeeeeeeeeeeee! Help Meeeeeeeeeeeeeeeeeee! Help Meeeeeeeeeeeeeeeeeee!"

"Oh aye," Vorik murmured, his man sac tightening. His acute silver gaze honed in on a mountain apex that looked to be a lengthy flight away. She was trapped alright—trapped and desperate to suckle a male nigh blind.

Vorik swallowed a bit roughly as he considered just how good of a suckling the dominant female was likely to give in her crazed, nigh unto starving state. Feeding her would like as naught kill him for she would demand great spurts to sate her.

His nostrils flared as he breathed in the crisp nighttime air. By the tit of the she-god, he was ready to die.

Fangs exploded into Vorik's mouth once again as he shot up from the ground, his body transforming into his *kor-tar* form as he leapt upwards.

He would find her in all haste.

He would feed her as any good master should.

He could not allow an alpha female to suffer from hunger pangs needlessly.

Ever thoughtful of others he was, he sniffed. Ever considerate of dimwitted creatures was he. Ever—

Bah! He wanted the she-beast to suck him dry. Enough said.

Chapter 3

Groggy with sleep, her eyelids firmly closed, Nancy's brow furrowed in incomprehension as she tried to figure out where the smooching sound she heard was coming from. It was a vaguely familiar noise, the type of kissy-fish lips, smooching, "here girl" kind of sound a person would make if they were calling a dog over to them that they might toss it a bone.

Her eyebrows shot up as she continued to sleep. Weird.

The sound was so bizarre to her in fact, so misplaced, that she rolled over onto her side with a grumble, and fell back into a deep, snoring sleep within seconds, her long skinny sword pressed against her backside.

Moments later she felt a large palm settle on her belly, then reverently run over the excess flesh there. Even in her sleep, her lips pinched together in a frown as she groggily considered the fact that even two months of dieting and exercise hadn't been enough to get rid of her belly. Or her thighs. Or her butt.

Damn it!

The feel of a solid piece of warm flesh tapping against her lips induced Nancy's forehead to crinkle bewilderedly. The tapping, accompanied by the kissy-fish lips "here girl" sound, was finally enough to rouse her from slumber and cause her eyelids to slowly flutter open.

Shit.

Nancy's eyes rounded in shock as she gaped up at the huge man kneeling down beside her. She had never—*never*—seen a man so gargantuan as this one. His body, which looked ominously long even kneeling down, was so thick with muscle that she wouldn't have been surprised if he weighed in the vicinity of five hundred pounds. He wasn't burly or stocky in the slightest, for his musculature looked right on him, but he was incredibly big in every way.

Tap. Tap. Tap.

Tap — tap.

Tap — tap — tap — tap.

Tap.

"Whadddyaddnd." Unable to part her lips to speak without a surprise visitor sneaking entrance inside, her nostrils flared incredulously as the big oaf continually tapped the head of his—extremely well endowed!—penis against the swell of her lips. The gargantuan's own lips were still pursed in kissy-fish form as he slapped his manhood against her, while the "here girl" sound he was emitting grew louder and more demanding.

The giant was treating her as if she were a dog and his penis a big bone to salivate over. Her nostrils flared even further. This was just too much.

Damn it!

What in the hell was going on? she mentally wailed. Who was this man? Where, she grumbled under her breath, had that witch whisked her off to? One thing was for certain, she hesitantly conceded, she had never—not even once—seen a man so large as this one in all of her life. She wasn't sure it was even genetically *possible* for a human male to be so gargantuan in size.

Frightened, Nancy's eyes flew up to meet the giant's, the expression on her face indignant regardless to the scare he was giving her. Never show fear, she staunchly told herself, remembering what she'd once heard on an Oprah show about deterring a possible assailant. Never show fear.

Tap – tap – tap.

Tap – tap.

Tap – tap – tap.

Unfortunately, she grimly conceded as the head of his cock kept up its tempo against her lips, her lack of exhibited fear didn't seem to be impressing him all that much. And—eek!—she really wished he'd quit making that kissy-fish lips sound.

Damn it!

* * * * *

Vorik landed softly upon two feet in the Khan-Gori perch, shape-shifting into his humanoid form whilst he entered the nest. His fangs retreated, his eyes shifted back from red to silver, and the wings seemingly dissolved from his back as the beast submerged in favor of the man.

His breath caught when he saw her lying stretched out under animal hides in the middle of the nest, her saucy silver sword-like tail erect even whilst slumbering. There she was in all her suckling glory. The plump alpha female he'd tracked—and caught.

"Oh aye you like to feed," he murmured, his muscles clenching in anticipation as his eyes drank in her fertile form. He bent down beside her, kneeling close to her slumbering body as he brushed away the animal pelts, and ran a large hand over the soft skin of her full underbelly.

She was fleshy, the dominant female was, and her love of eating was proof positive that she was to become a pet he would cherish and pamper for all time.

Vorik closed his eyes briefly and took a steadying breath, for he was embarrassingly close to spurting before the *yenni* was even roused enough to suckle of him. His cock was as long and hard as 'twas possible for it to be and his man sac was so tight that the excruciatingly exquisite feeling bordered on pain.

By the tit of the she-god, her chubby form was nigh unto driving him daft with arousal.

Pursing his lips together, his cock in hand, Vorik announced the arrival of a hearty meal to the dimwitted *yenni* with the traditional sound a male of his species makes in such a situation as he tapped the head of his staff against her lips, beckoning to her to eat. When her eyes fluttered open—by the ice of Mount Shalor they were beautiful!—he was certain 'twas the need of a meal he saw in her rounded gaze.

He tapped his cock harder against her mouth, nigh unto desperate for her suctioning lips to part. Sweat dotted his brow as he willed her mouth to open, as he prayed to the mating gods for surcease.

Oh aye, he thought headily as his man sac tightened impossibly more, her nostrils were flaring, inhaling the scent of food no doubt. More aroused than he'd thought it possible for himself to become, his teeth gritted and his muscles clenched anticipatorily as he tapped his cock harder still against her lips.

She would part them eventually, he knew, for the lure of a hot meal would be too tempting to resist o'er long.

Vorik's eyes flicked o'er her fleshy underbelly, grazed o'er her full hips and breasts.

Oh aye, he told himself as his eyes glazed o'er in need, eventually the alpha female would part her suctioning lips.

And when she did, she would feed.

* * * * *

"Whaddydndg?" Nancy asked furiously, her lips firmly clamped shut. She ignored the heated stare his silver eyes gave back to her and, huffing, pushed his manhood away from her face as she came up on her knees. "What," she bit out, her teeth set, "are you doing?"

Oh no, she thought, her forcefulness wavering a bit. His eyes—his damn eyes. They were…silver. Not grey, not light blue, not some murky could-be-human color, but sharp, piercing, acute…silver.

She gulped, scooting back a bit out of reflex.

The giant's breathing hitched just a little as his gaze meandered up and down her body. Naked on her knees before him, his piercing silver eyes seemed to meld as they flicked over her face, then down lower to her breasts, lower still to her tummy, and even lower yet to her…

"Shit," Nancy muttered, biting down on her lip. She backed up a bit more, scurrying away as quickly as one could while on their knees. She had forgotten she was naked. How could she have forgotten that she was—

Gggggggrrrrrr

She gasped when the giant began to growl low in his throat, the sound he was emitting telling her without words that if she knew what was good for her, then she had best not move another inch away from him. Her jaw agape, her mind frenziedly trying to figure out a method of escape, she unthinkingly scooted further away from him until she had all but trapped herself against the far wall of the nest.

"Oh my—eek!" Nancy's hands shot up to cover her ears as his low growl evolved into a blood-curdling roar of anger. Her gaze widened and she gasped again when his eyes shifted from silver to dull-glowing crimson, fangs simultaneously exploding from his gums to expose incisors long enough to make a woman swoon.

Her hands fell down to her sides, numb. She really should have taken that job in Anchorage.

Silver eyes that turn red, she thought in dawning horror, growls that become roars, fangs that...well he had fangs!

Hysterically deciding she at last knew how Fay Wray had felt when King Kong had plucked her from the sacrificial altar on Skull Island, she backed up on her knees all the way against the far wall of the nest while her hands instinctively flew up to shield her ears once again. "Heeeelp mmmeeeeeeeeeeeeee!"

Oddly, those shrieked out words seem to calm him, even satisfy him. "Huh?" Nancy's eyebrows shot up uncomprehendingly, wondering as she did why he'd had such a positive reaction to the shrill sound of her wailing.

The giant's eyes shifted back from crimson to silver, and his fangs retreated below the gumline as though they'd never been. The muscles in his huge—and naked!—body seemed to clench as he stood up...up...way up...and slowly inched his way towards her.

She harrumphed. He was grasping his penis by the base again and making those damned kissy-fish noises as he arrogantly strode to stand before her kneeling form. He was beckoning to her again, calling out to her as though she was a dog and he was offering her a supreme cut of beef.

Damn it!

She swept a hand about grandly, purposely ignoring the horrific manner in which the nest was beginning to teeter back and forth. "Forget it," she sniffed. "It won't happen. Not now. Not—*eek!*"

Nancy screamed loud enough to wake the dead as the giant's added weight caused the nest to teeter too far to the side—far enough that she got a bone-chilling look at how far she'd be plummeting to her death if he came any closer. Her heart rate soared. Sweat broke out all over her body. "Okay!" she shrieked, her breasts heaving up and down. "You win! For the love of God you win, but please quit moving!"

Either he was purposely ignoring her words or he couldn't understand what she was saying, but either way the giant kept prowling toward her, cock in hand. Nancy panicked when she felt the nest sway down lower, and with a scream, she lunged up at the gargantuan male and jumped into his heavily muscled embrace, her only objective to keep him in the middle of the nest that the structure would remain perched upright.

The giant laughed as he effortlessly caught her, dimples popping out on either cheek as he plucked her out of mid-air like a trite leaf and grinned down into her face.

Their eyes clashed. Nancy's breath caught.

Damn he was handsome, she thought rather warily, not at all liking the fact that her skin felt tingly and alive when it brushed up against the giant ogre's. In fact, she felt more than alive and tingly—she felt downright turned on. Huh?

Damn it!

Nancy chewed on her lower lip as she studied him, an odd and completely out of place premonition that everything would be okay swamping her senses. He wouldn't hurt her—not like that, not sexually. Her forehead crinkled as she idly wondered how she could remain so calm and sure given the situation. But there it was. She *was* sure.

And there was another feeling there as well, a gut instinct that shot through her and permeated her consciousness as her brown eyes shot up once more to meet his molten silver ones.

She gulped roughly. She wasn't certain how she knew, didn't know what instinct or intuition was guiding her thoughts, but she was sure of one thing: the witch didn't plan to let her leave this place or this giant.

Ever.

Chapter 4

Nancy swallowed nervously as the giant laid her down upon her back and settled his huge form next to hers. He curled his muscled body around her in such a way that her face was kept close to his swollen penis. Her breath came out in a rush, and she was surprised to find that her body was reacting fiercely to his.

But it wasn't the need to suckle him that was making her feel breathless and passionate, though she could ascertain that was precisely what the giant wanted from her! It was the need to mate with the huge predator that was arousing her so fiercely. She didn't just want to have sex with him, she thought uneasily, she wanted to actually mate with him, to have him implant his child in her womb…

"Oh lord," she whimpered, her nipples hardening, her breath coming out in pants. She knew something wasn't right, wasn't as it should be. Human women do not react to human males like…like…good grief like dogs in heat. But that's exactly what she felt like, and what's worse, she could swear she felt every egg that lined her ovaries tingling, waiting to be fertilized.

Damn it!

Nancy groaned, clamping a hand to her forehead as she did so. What in the name of God was happening to her? she thought morosely, her lips forming a dramatic martyr's slash. What manner of…species…was this fanged predator that he could make her body react so damned primitively?

Her stomach rumbled, reminding her she hadn't eaten in an age. She'd been too keyed up at Lori's party to consume a morsel, and too worried about her waistline expanding to take a bite. But now…

Nancy's eyes flicked up to the giant's face as her breathing grew increasingly sporadic. Now, she thought worriedly as her eyes locked with his and she saw his breathing hitch, now she was hungry.

* * * * *

Vorik heard the *yenni* groan, the sound followed immediately by the noise of her empty belly rumbling.

Oh aye, he thought shakily, his man sac tightening til 'twas nigh unto blue, at long last the alpha female was hungered enough to dine upon him. Every muscle in his body clenched in anticipation, and his breath came out in a rush when her dimwitted eyes flew up to meet with his. That an intelligence seemed to lurk behind the dominant female's gaze was of no interest to him at this juncture, for all he could think on was the fact that after having been forced to wait so many agonizing years for bodily surcease, his cock was about to be suckled of seed.

He reached out and brushed a lock of hair away from her face. Verily, he had never seen hair the color of hers, a soft amber hue that made his heart ache.

The color of her bedamned hair made his heart ache? Arrg! By the tit of the she-god, he would not fall in love with a dimwitted *yenni*. Verily, he frowned, 'twould make him the laughingstock of his entire pack!

Vorik saw the hesitation in her eyes and wondered at it. Mayhap a former master had treated her badly, he thought sadly, his heart constricting yet further. His teeth gritted as he steeled himself against his emotions, yet he found that all the steeling in the galaxies could not keep his heart from thumping madly in tune with hers.

Ah well no matter, he assured himself, 'twas probably a normal reaction any male of his species had to the first pet he captured. Mayhap a Barbarian always holds a special place in his heart for the she-beast who's the first to suckle of him. 'Twas a passing fancy, that.

The heaving of her breasts caught his attention, inducing Vorik's hand to instinctively reach out and palm one. 'Twas large and full, he thought wonderingly, his breath hitching once more. He ran his thumb o'er the elongated rouge nipple, then closed his eyes briefly whilst he dragged in a calming breath at the sound of her gasp of pleasure.

Her nipples were like *maji* fruits, he thought as his nostrils flared. Puffy at the base, long and ripe at the peak.

Vorik's silver eyes bore into the *yenni's*, the troubled look within her dark gaze still causing his heart to ache. He continued to stroke her silken mane of hair, his eyes gentling at her worried expression. His other hand reached further down her body until his thumb found her clit. He massaged it gently to soothe her. "Sha nala faron, zya." *'Twill be alright, little one.* He smiled softly. "Khan-Gori m'alana fey." *I will not harm you.*

She looked as though she understood not what his words meant, which Vorik had expected since all *yenni* were dim of the mind, yet he could tell that the gentle way he'd spoken the words had calmed her fears a bit. Her eyes flicked down to his shaft, no doubt remembering the need of a meal, and he felt his man sac go entirely blue as it tightened further, ready to explode for her.

And then, oh aye and then, the alpha female gave herself up to the lure of a hot meal as her lips slowly clamped around the sensitive head of his manhood. Vorik groaned at the first touch, his muscles cording when he saw and felt her suctioning lips envelop the head in its entirety.

"Oh aye," he moaned hoarsely, perspiration dotting his brow, wetting his shoulder-length black hair. His breathing grew labored as he watched her eyes close, as he heard her softly moan whilst she began attending to his cock. A rush of air came out from his lungs in a hiss as he gently guided her head up and down his shaft, his fingers twined through her hair as he pressed her closer to him.

She suckled him ferociously, getting more and more into the feeding as her eyes closed and she worked her suctioning lips vigorously up and down his staff. Her nipples hardened as she toyed with him, as she did what the females of her species had done since the advent of time to males of his species.

Vorik groaned when her small hands began massaging his man sac, gasping when he knew he was nigh close unto bursting already. Her ravenous tongue knew how to flick about his sensitive head, her nimble fingers knew just how much pressure to apply to his scrotum. He gasped again as he watched his cock disappear into the depths of her mouth, her eyes closed in bliss as she suckled up and down the length of him.

She took him in a frenzy, her suctioning mouth working faster and faster, the sound of lips meeting cock smacking throughout the nest. Vorik growled low in his throat, unable to stop his fangs from emerging from his gums. He cradled her head reverently at his groin, his silver eyes opening then narrowing in crimson desire as he watched her feast on him.

She suckled faster, then faster still, her silken amber head bobbing up and down upon his manhood. When her tiny hands began massaging his man sac in earnest in time with her sucks, his head fell back upon the animal hides and his muscles corded. She seemed to know 'twas time to make him spurt, for her suctioning mouth honed in on the sensitive head and she sucked upon it greedily whilst massaging his tight balls.

Oh aye, Vorik thought, his mind nigh unto delirious. 'Twas bliss, this.

His entire body shuddered, then clenched hotly in anticipation of release. The *yenni* continued to work the magic of her kind upon him harder and harder still, her fingers massaging his scrotum whilst her lips pulled, sucked, and suctioned at the sensitive head.

"Zya," he roared. Vorik exploded between her lips, his fangs jutting fully into his mouth whilst his entire body shuddered and convulsed. She groaned as his seed spurted into her mouth, then closed her eyes as she fed from him, lapping up every last glowing drop of his silvery dew.

It was long minutes before he could catch his breath and even longer minutes before he could see again, for stars had exploded behind his eyes when he'd spurted and he had felt nigh close unto swooning from the intensity of his release. But at last, when finally he was able to steady himself and breathe normally again, he gazed down upon her lush form and his man sac instantly tightened for her.

Oh aye, he thought headily, a smile of contentment pervading his lips as he nudged her face with gentle reverence back down toward his groin, this *yenni* was a hungry alpha without a doubt.

She studied him with an astonished expression for a few moments, her eyes clashing with his as she apparently decided what to do. But eventually, just as Vorik had thought she would—as he'd hoped she would—the beautiful, hungry she-beast latched her lips around the head of his manhood again and began the process of feeding from him all o'er again.

Vorik laid back upon the *muu* animal hides with a dreamy sigh, his heavily muscled arms flung o'er his head in surrender to her appetite. He closed his eyes and smiled blissfully as her lips worked o'er him once more, praying that 'twould take many sucklings before her belly felt full.

Verily, he thought on a gasp as his man sac tightened with seed, who needed a Bloodmate when a pet so fine as this one needed food.

Still, he was no saint, he knew. Aye he enjoyed feeding her, but 'twould be bliss when she'd had her fill and he could stuff his cock into her wet, puffed up pussy.

Oh aye. 'Twould be bliss.

* * * * *

Nancy wasn't sure if she'd gone insane or not, but four blowjobs later she decided that she had. Her jaw was so sore it was throbbing, yet every time the huge predator gazed down at her with stars in his eyes she'd find her lips latching around his penis of seemingly their own accord and she'd begin the process of making him come all over again.

She sighed resignedly, realizing as she did that it was heady indeed to have a male gaze down at you as though you were a goddess. That the male doing the gazing was the most handsome and powerful man she'd ever laid eyes on only added to the giddiness. She knew he was young—he had to be young regardless of his gigantic size, for his reaction to her touching was completely unschooled and…naively touching.

As he spurted the sweetest liquid she'd ever tasted into her mouth for a body-shattering fifth time, she told herself that she had to be dreaming. He was eight feet tall, he had to weigh five hundred pounds or more, his eyes were silver when he was sated and crimson when he was angry or passionate, he had fangs, and he growled.

Definitely not what one would call a lucid reality.

And yet, weird as it was, she knew deep down inside that she wasn't dreaming. She knew that she was awake, and that this gargantuan male would do all in his power to keep her from escaping him.

She felt a pang of fear course through her as she wondered what she could do to get away from him. He was handsome for sure, but handsome wasn't enough to keep her from wanting to go home.

But if she did find a way to escape while he was sleeping or otherwise unaware, what then? Nancy sighed as she laid down beside him, her head coming down to rest upon his chest, her mind too tired to reason out any escape attempts just now.

She had no idea where she was and no idea how to leave it behind. Where the witch had thrown her to she could only guess.

Jaid Black

Chapter 5

Vorik awoke in the silvery twilight with a tight man sac, the need to mate weighing down upon him mightily. He smiled as he cuddled his pet closer, the sound of her contented snoring causing him to chuckle.

Aye, she had fed well on him last moon-rising. Verily, she had suckled him nigh blind just as he'd hoped she would.

He sighed dreamily, his eyes still closed, as his large hand ran down her lush backside to play with her tail whilst she slumbered. She was perfection, his pet. She was an exuberant suckler who would bring him many lifetimes of bliss. She was—

His brow furrowed as his hand fumbled about her backside. Where was her tail? he grumbled to himself. He felt no appendage at all there. Surely his pet had to have a tail! Where was...

"Ahh gods."

Vorik's eyes flew open and darted downward, his silver gaze clashing with an intelligent brown one. His eyes narrowed as he looked at her, really looked at her for the first time, and apparently his intense study of her features frightened her for she swallowed nervously and looked away.

By the Ices of Shalor, he thought with surprise, the female was no *yenni* at all. She was humanoid—a humanoid wench. Ahh gods what a dunce he was! He grimaced. Now that he viewed her in the harsh light of day she had naught in common with a *yenni* other than creamy, pearly skin. She was too beautiful to be a *yenni*, and her eyes were too knowing.

But nay, Vorik silently qualified, he was not one known for being a lackwit. He could have sworn she'd had a tail when first he'd ensnared her—aye she'd had a tail. Hadn't she?

Well no matter, he grunted, his palm kneading the backside he refused to relinquish—humanoid or no. Whether she'd had a tail or his eyes had been playing tricks on him was irrelevant just now, for he knew with all certainty she had let loose the cry of an alpha female *yenni* desirous of a feeding. That much of last moon-rising's events was a certainty.

He grunted again, satisfied in his reasoning, contented in realizing he was no dunce. Feeling amorous as his species was want to do, he plucked the humanoid wench from her lying position and set her upon his lap that her legs straddled him. She yelped a bit at first, her large breasts heaving up and down, and he figured correctly that she was frightened of his size.

Well no matter. He would gentle her to his touch, then would he do the very deed he'd been nigh dying to do since he'd been a twelve-year-old pup.

Slowly, Vorik's dark head came up and his sharp silver eyes clashed with her rich dark ones. She swallowed nervously, looking away from him again, which was just as well for his mouth had dropped open in shock.

By the tit of the she-god, his sins were worse than he'd thought!

Vorik groaned, sorely vexed with himself. His cheeks pinkened in embarrassment and shame as he considered the reality of what he'd done. Not only was she no *yenni*, not only was she a humanoid, but she was something far more important and coveted than either of those things. She was the very elusive dream most males of his species spent lifetimes searching for and, sadly, many never found. She was his—all his—and no other's. And he'd found her on the very moon-rising he'd become a Barbarian full grown.

"Oh aye," he murmured as he felt his body respond to hers, as the need to mount her and impregnate her womb instinctually kicked in. Every cell in his body tingled as he drank in the scent of her. His manhood hardened with thoughts of gorging upon her blood...and, oh aye, with tantalizing thoughts of her gorging upon his blood.

Vorik released a shaky breath as his hands clutched her hips and his fingers dug into the flesh there. He needed to mate her now, to sink himself deep inside of her and get a litter of pups on her the soonest.

By the gods, she was his Bloodmate.

* * * * *

Nancy gasped when, in the blink of an eye, he reversed their positions and lowered his massive body between her comparatively small legs. She sighed, thinking it had taken being thrown into another world—most likely another planet entirely!—for her to feel small and delicate next to a man. A fanged man. A fanged man with a penis large enough to rend her into halves.

"EEEK!" Nancy pushed at the unmoving wall that was his chest, her legs flailing madly at either side of his hips. She hadn't been able to get even half of his shaft into her mouth last night—there was no way in the hell it was going between her legs.

"Forget it!" she fumed, her voice indignant. "The buck stops here, buddy." For a woman who had been a spinster all of a day ago, this was just too much. Sucking on him was one thing—and she still wasn't certain what had possessed her to do that much!—but having him put it inside of her was another thing altogether. She bet he'd never once suffered from a case of penis envy. No locker room ribbings for this guy. Her hand slashed definitively through the air. "There is no way you will ever—eek!"

A growl of outrage erupted from his throat as fangs exploded through his gums. His once silver eyes turned crimson in anger, in lust, in possessiveness. He was anxious to get inside of her—very anxious she knew when he bent his head and nipped at her shoulder disapprovingly. She wondered if all the fighting in the world would keep him from sinking into her, which she feared could possibly kill her!

And yet, as anxious as she could tell he was to dominate her will and her body, he stilled himself atop her, waiting for...something. Waiting for her to calm herself, perhaps?

Nancy's lips pinched together in a frown as she considered the fact that his method was working. She *was* becoming calmer. And the moonstruck way that he was gazing down at her, the same worshipping, hopeful expression that King Kong had harbored as he'd watched Fay Wray's every movement, was doing its damnedest to work a number on her senses.

She sighed, her eyes closing and her hands coming up to rub at her temples. This was weirdness incarnate. The ultimate getting-kidnapped-by-a-mountain-man scenario. And what's worse, she had a perverse feeling that by the time all was said and done, she'd have become a willing captive.

Damn it!

Her nostrils flaring, Nancy's eyes flew open to meet her captor's and their gazes locked. He looked ferocious. Determined. His jaw was set, his fangs slightly bared, and his eyes were now pure crimson.

Oh damn, she thought as she began panting, she could feel him telepathically speaking into her mind. She had no idea what he was saying because she couldn't speak his tongue, but whatever the words were they were doing a number on her hormonally. She groaned as horniness the likes of which she'd never before felt shuddered through her, then gasped when her womb began to contract.

She needed his flesh joined to hers, needed to feel him rocking in and out of her, needed him to impregnate her. She would obey him in all things, she thought unblinkingly, for she could do no other. She belonged to him forever. Verily, her body was but his vessel, ever ready to provide pleasure—

"Damn it!" she sniffed. Her eyes narrowed when she realized he'd been hypnotizing her. "Quit making me think things I don't want to think!"

He smiled slowly as an answer, then sent out a sensual mental wave that left her gaping like the village idiot.

Nancy closed her eyes and moaned, her body involuntarily writhing beneath the giant's. Good grief, she silently wailed, she was back to feeling like a dog in heat only this time the effect was a thousand times worse—and likely to drive her mad if he didn't enter her body soon.

"Please," she groaned, her breaths coming out in a series of short gasps. To hell with worries about dying, she sniffed. She needed him inside of her like she needed to breathe. She decided this was no time to contemplate how troublesome of a fact that was. She wrapped her legs around his waist without thinking about it, then reared up her hips and ground her soaking wet flesh against his groin.

He hissed.

"*Please.*"

He settled himself comfortably between her legs, then bent his dark head to nip at her neck with his teeth. Not enough to drink of her, but enough to puncture the skin and to cause a few droplets of her blood to trickle out onto his tongue. He lapped the beads of blood up, groaning as if she tasted like an elixir from the gods.

"Oh lord," she groaned, her belly knotting with impending climax, "oh yes." She felt delirious—good grief what was he doing to her?

She didn't know what instinct made her bite him, couldn't say what drove her to it, but in a frenzy of lust and intuition, Nancy's head shot up and she clamped down onto his jugular vein as hard as she could with her comparatively dull teeth. He began to writhe and moan, his low growl evolving into a fierce roar.

Incisors sliced cleanly into her jugular, causing her to whimper from the human fear of death mingled with an evolving predator's ecstasy. She never let go of his jugular, though, and soon she would be glad she hadn't.

An orgasm exploded inside of her as he drank her blood, the violence of it intense enough to make her body involuntarily convulse. Amidst the throes of a full mating frenzy, it didn't matter that Nancy's incisors were dull in comparison to the teeth of the male who was preparing to mount her. Her human teeth sank into his jugular as far as they could go, and although they couldn't go far enough to drink of him they were able to go in far enough to nick him, which caused him to bleed a single droplet of blood.

It was enough. The moment the sweet taste of his blood hit her tongue, Nancy groaned as her body convulsed with yet another orgasm. She enjoyed the intensity so much that even when he made her release his neck so he could mount her the way he wanted to, she bit down onto his chest and drew blood, refusing to let go, moaning and groaning when orgasm after orgasm rocked through her.

"Oh aye, little one," he said hoarsely.

Her body stilled. Her teeth fell away from his chest as reality set in. She was drinking a man's blood.

"Oh God," she dramatically wailed.

"I need to mount you, *vorah*," the giant said thickly, seemingly unaware of her tumultuous thoughts. His silver eyes glazed over as he nudged her down to lie fully upon her back. He then settled himself on his knees between her legs, clutching her hips with his hands and spreading her thighs wide.

"Wh-what are y-you doing?"

What a dumb question!

"Mounting you," he said in a hoarse voice.

Eeeek!

Against her volition, Nancy's nipples hardened and elongated as she watched the gargantuan-sized predator prepare to thrust inside of her for the first time. Eyes closed and nostrils flaring, she could tell by the look of impending nirvana smothering his features that the eight-foot giant getting ready to mate her had never been with another woman. Never.

A five-hundred pound virgin. A five-hundred pound virgin who drinks blood and possesses a penis the size of a small whale.

Eeeek!

"Oh dear," she whimpered, her logical mind at war with her eyes—eyes that were busy drinking in the intoxicating sight of his heavily muscled body. Why did her body react to him as if it had been preprogrammed to? "P-Perhaps we should start slower," she hedged, glancing uneasily up at his fangs. "Maybe holding hands would be nice—"

She said no more when he looked at her as though she'd gone mad. Good lord she probably had gone mad! That certainly explained this new world she was inhabiting. Perhaps she and the other mental wards at the local asylum were visiting here at the same time. Right after they'd had tea with Napoleon. Nervously, her hand darted up to push the spectacles she always wore up the bridge of her nose. Oh that's right. She wasn't wearing any spectacles.

Damn it!

Nancy closed her eyes and groaned, a melodramatic feeling of martyrdom overtaking her. What was so wrong with being a spinster? she mentally wailed. Why had she ever thought to get a new life?

"'Twill be alright, little one," he murmured. "Verily, I could never hurt you."

Her eyes flew open. For the first time it dawned on her she could understand what he was saying. And, she thought bewilderedly, he wasn't speaking English by any stretch of the imagination. "H-How…"

"Thine blood is in me." He bent his head and sipped at her neck again, causing her to gasp. "And mine in you," he murmured.

Her breath caught when, with no more preliminaries, he raised her hips up a bit, then impaled himself within her flesh in one long, arousing stroke. It hadn't killed her after all. "Oh my," she gasped, her back arching.

"*Vorah*," he ground out, sweat dotting his brow, "I've the need to rut in you, little one."

Vorah—Bloodmate…the human equivalent to wife.

Oh lord.

Nancy gazed up at the gigantic male whose flesh was fully embedded in hers and was surprised by the array of emotions she felt just looking at him. It worried her really, for it meant that not only had her body been preprogrammed to need him, but her heart had been as well. But preprogrammed by whom? By what? She sighed, very confused.

Vorik stroked into her flesh slowly once more, the look of rapture on his face heady enough to tug at Nancy's heartstrings. She closed her eyes briefly, opening them on a sigh, the poignant feeling of being his first lover doing a tap dance on her emotions…and her libido. She actually found herself wishing that she knew what to call him by.

Vorik, he answered in her mind. *Thy Bloodmate*.

Their eyes met. Nancy nibbled at her lower lip as her reticence dissolved.

"I'm Nancy," she whispered.

Vorik entered her slowly again, groaning as he seated himself fully within her. "Nawncy," he ground out. He held her thighs apart with his large hands, his hips rotating in between them as he thrust into her flesh.

She gasped, her nipples hardening.

Vorik bent his head to her chest, his tongue darting out to curl around one jutting nipple. Nancy moaned loudly, for his tongue was rough like a cat's and the gentle sandpaper sensation sent tremors shooting through her. He sucked on the nipple for a long time while he slowly thrust into her, and pretty soon she was so wet that she could hear her pussy making sucking sounds with every slow upstroke.

He flicked at her nipple with his tongue, then raised his dark head. "Are you ready for more, beautiful one?" he murmured.

"Yes," she gasped, her hips arching up to meet his next downstroke.

He closed his eyes and picked up the pace, thrusting into her flesh in deep, wild strokes, moaning and groaning the entire time. Sweat broke out onto his forehead. The muscles in his arms clenched and corded. His teeth gritted as he rode her into oblivion, never wanting the sensations to end.

Nancy watched his face the entire time, moaning as he took her. It was a heady feeling, owning the first pussy a man ever fucked. The expression on his face was indescribable in its intensity. He looked delirious with pleasure, yet she could tell from the way his jaw was clenched as he rocked in and out of her that he was doing his damnedest to keep from orgasming. He wanted the euphoria to last. He never wanted to stop fucking her.

She moaned when he rode her harder, his hips pistoning faster and faster between her thighs. She could hear her flesh sucking him in, trying to hold onto his cock every time he rocked back and forth.

"Aye," she heard him growl. His eyes were closed, as if concentrating intently on the feel of her cunt. He mounted her primally, holding back nothing.

Harder. Deeper. Faster. *"Aye."*

Nancy gasped as incisors sliced cleanly into her neck. She came instantaneously, screaming as she threw her hips back at him.

With a growl he gorged on her, feeding on her blood as he stuffed his stiff cock inside of her over and over, again and again. He moaned and groaned throughout every last orgasm, allowing her as much pleasure as he could, taking from her as much pleasure as he could, before the deed was fully done and he wouldn't be able to touch her whilst she incubated.

When she came again—writhing and moaning, throwing her hips at him like a wanton—he could take no more torture. Raising one finger to his neck, he allowed the nail to spike up, then slashed open his jugular and lowered it to her.

She drank of him, became one with him, never thought to deny him. He roared at the euphoric sensation of her feasting on him, the feeling akin to never-ending orgasmic release.

Only when Vorik knew the deed was done, when he was certain she'd drank enough of him to evolve, did he allow himself the final, harsh release. Realizing as he did that he would not get to make love to her for a sennight, he glutted on her blood and cunt as long as 'twas possible, hedonistically enjoying every sip, every thrust.

"*Vorah.*"

He came on a loud roar, his eyes crimson with passion, with possession. The orgasm went on and on and on, 'til finally his man sac had been emptied of all seed.

When it was over, when both of their breathing returned to normal, Vorik smiled down at her, his expression worshipful. "Many thanks, little one," he murmured. "'Twas more bliss than I can say."

Nancy grinned. "You weren't too bad your…" She gasped, as she felt her breath slowly leave her body. "Vorik," she panted, "what the…"

He smiled. "You are evolving, my love." He disentangled his body from hers so as to not impede the process. "'Twill be but one sennight in the cocoon—"

"C-Cocoon?" she cried out. Gasping for air, she rolled onto her side, noticing for the first time that a web was forming around her hands—a thick web of sticky material. *"Oh my God."*

She screamed, trying to bat the web away with her hands, but it was growing and thickening, and climbing up her arms. "Help me!" she screamed, jumping up to her feet. She gasped as more air left her lungs, then fell to her knees.

Nancy watched in dawning horror as the web made it's way up her arms and began encasing her fully, all the way down to her toes. Unable to scream from a lack of oxygen in her lungs, she mentally screamed, rolling and rolling, and rolling her body to the far side of the nest.

Vorik came after her, not wanting her to harm her cocoon lest she die. *"Vorah!"* he commanded her. "Calm thyself and quit moving anon!"

But Nancy was delirious, wild, frantic. She rolled further, and Vorik stepped closer. The nest teetered and swayed.

"Vorah!"

Cold terror knifed through her as the nest collapsed and she began plummeting toward the ground at a bone chilling speed. She bypassed winged animals, mountain peaks, and—oh God—a mountain base, as she plummeted down, down, down, down...

She was almost completely encased, nothing but her eyes showing as the cocoon turned over so Nancy could see up instead of down.

Vorik.

He was coming after her, swooping down from the heavens. But he was no longer a man.

Silver body. Silver wings. Fangs. Crimson eyes...

Nancy silently screamed as the cocoon encased her fully, her last conscious thought before her breath left her entirely that the man she'd just made love to was a gargoyle.

And worse...he had turned her into one too.

* * * * *

Vorik swooped down and caught the *vorah*-sac in his arms, careful not to snag it with his teeth as was the automatic instinct possessed by his kind when in *kor-tar* form. But then usually when one was descending upon a body 'twas as a predator seizing prey so he cared not whether his fangs ripped through the animal's flesh. Since this was the cocoon of his evolving Bloodmate, however, he cared mightily.

He cradled the *vorah*-sac in his arms, cautious of her delicate state at all times. She was defenseless just now, unable to protect herself whilst she incubated, and so 'twas her Bloodmate she depended upon at this time for safety more so than she ever would again.

When Nancy awoke, he knew the metabolic changes within would cause her to be as deadly as was he—mayhap even more so—for he'd never heard tell of a species of predators in any dimension where the female wasn't deadlier than the male. Mayhap 'twas to compensate for the fact that she would be much smaller than a lot of the species of prey they would stalk together throughout their seven lifetimes together.

There were many characteristics that the Barbarians of Khan-Gor shared in common with other predators, the most fundamental one being the difference between the genders. Although Nancy would be gifted with the ability to kill attackers and seize prey in many deadly ways that Vorik could not, she would never be able to best her own Bloodmate—never.

Vorik smiled at that thought, thinking the gods showed much in the way of smarts. Verily, if the deadly female was able to bring the male she had mated with down, then males would be killed off left and right, mayhap every time their *vorahs* got into a temper. Since Bloodmates mated for life, 'twould be foolhardy of nature to allow for such, for the predator populace would die out and those lower on the foodchain would become too great in numbers.

And so it had come to pass through the long process of evolution that the Khan-Gori male was possessed of two gifts the female was not: whilst in animal form his silver skin was impenetrable from puncture wounds dealt by a Bloodmate, and whilst in either form he could mesmerize his Bloodmate should he so desire it. Those two attributes, working in conjunction with his larger, fiercer size, gave the Khan-Gori male eternal dominion o'er his deadly *vorah*.

Vorik dismissed his stray thoughts as he scanned the grounds and mountain passes for a safe place to make camp til the sennight of incubation had passed and his Bloodmate emerged from her cocoon. He couldn't chance flying all the way back to F'al Vader lands this way with her in his arms, for if a rival predator made battle with him, he would be forced to choose between dropping the *vorah*-sac to fight—which would kill Nancy in the process, or allowing himself to be killed by a male from another pack. Since Vorik would choose to die with his Bloodmate rather than drop her, he knew 'twould mean death to them both.

His crimson eyes located an empty cavern below which his visual acuity told him was not currently being inhabited. He swooped down to make haste toward it, realizing as he did from years worth of hunting that the cavern was nestled within neutral lands unclaimed by any pack. 'Twould do.

Vorik sent out a mental warning to weaker lifeforms below that did they wish to see the next morn, they would clear out the cavern immediately until he and his Bloodmate left it behind. His acute hearing picked up the vibrations of scampering feet and, verily, by the time he arrived with his *vorah*-sac and had shape-shifted to humanoid form, all signs of life were long gone.

He carried Nancy into the ice-coated cavern, his Bloodmate securely cradled in his arms.

Chapter 6
One week later

Nancy's breath came back in a rush, her lungs heaving and expelling a huge gush of air. Crimson eyes flew open and fangs exploded from her gums as she instinctively sought out her Bloodmate. In a behavior pattern that had genetically been programmed into her during the incubation period, she exploded from the cocoon with a fierce roar, able to do so by a lining of deadly spikes that jutted out of the skin cells on her forearms.

Unable to think of anything save the need for Vorik's nearness, and voraciously aroused after having not mated during the entire week she'd been cocooned, Nancy flew at top speed out of the cavern, her heightened sense of smell detecting that Vorik was a mile off, somewhere in the vicinity of the mouth of the icy riverbed below.

The scent of him aroused her further, inducing her nipples to harden and her belly to knot in anticipation of being mounted. The moment her Bloodmate saw her descending upon him, his lips formed a snarl as he shape-shifted into *kor-tar* form and took flight towards her.

Their silver bodies came together in a mid-air clash, and Vorik immediately sank his teeth into her neck. Nancy gasped at the arousal, her need to be impregnated by the large male too instinctual to resist him. That he now looked like a gargoyle, that he was fanged and winged and his eyes were crimson — all of these things her earthly memory cells were wary of, but the need to couple was too pressing to pay them much heed.

As her Bloodmate lowered them to the ground with a fierce growl, then forced her bodily onto her hands and knees, she could think of nothing—*nothing*—but being mounted. It was as if she'd never been human, as if her body harbored no memories of an existence before she'd emerged from the cocoon.

On a dangerous growl Vorik entered her from behind, his thick swollen penis impaling her warm flesh in one thrust. She hissed at his roughness, glancing over her shoulder to snarl at him. He growled in response, then nipped at her shoulder with his teeth to show her who was in control as he pounded into her cunt from behind. She yipped in response, whimpering like a puppy who'd had her tail stepped on at the chastisement.

Vorik immediately soothed her, his tongue darting out to lap at her shoulder while he kept up his steady tempo of thrusts. Nancy gasped in pleasure, then began to couple with him, throwing her hips back at him to increase the friction and the deepness.

Aye little one, she heard a hoarse voice in her mind say. *I've missed thy presence sorely. Fuck me with that sweet cunt.*

She did as he bade her, throwing her flesh back at him, moaning and groaning as he pounded into her body, hissing with ecstasy as his sharp fingernails dug into the flesh of her hips. She didn't understand why the sensation of his fingernails piercing her skin felt so good, only knew that it did. It was like a sensual massage, akin to the way it would feel if her clitoris was being rubbed.

On a growl she burst, her wet flesh contracting as she came. The orgasm was a thousand times stronger than anything she'd ever before experienced, causing her to moan and groan and writhe and twist as Vorik continued to impale her over and over again, his tight balls slapping against her buttocks while he frenziedly rutted inside of her.

Vorik, she mentally moaned.

I wish it to last, he answered, his teeth gritting, *I wish it to – ahh gods*.

On a loud roar he prepared to explode, the intense feeling of her pussy contracting around his cock forcing him into it. He had heard tell that a Bloodmate's cunt would suck a Khan-Gori male's staff dry, but not until now did he know that the gossip was true.

Verily, her flesh squeezed him in a series of intense contractions until he could withstand no more, until he was moaning and groaning and growling from the pleasure of it. Vorik pounded into her wet flesh twice more, then clawed her hips to force her into peaking with him as he emptied his seed deep inside of her.

For three more hours they mated thusly, over and over, again and again. With each mating Vorik became more animalistic, drinking her blood to heighten the delirious ecstasy for both of them, scratching at her hips to make her tremor and convulse around his cock.

He took her with the violence of his species, primal in a way he could never be while she was in her humanoid form. Only one time during the entire mating did she snarl at him to get off of her, and that was only after she'd been effectually impregnated with a pup and wanted some rest. Vorik, a virgin just a week ago, wanted more and more and more of her pussy, refusing to stop until he burst again and again inside of her.

When Nancy protested with a growl, his answering roar of denial followed by a sharp nick to the shoulder silenced her. Obediently, she pressed one side of her face to the ground and hoisted her hips up further that he might root in her as deeply and as much as he desired.

Vorik grunted in satisfaction, a snort of male arrogance puncturing the night as he impaled her flesh over and over again with his. Amidst a mating frenzy, he pummeled her roughly, mounting her for another solid hour, spurting seed into her flesh more times than either of them could count.

When finally he was sated, when his balls were drained of all seed, Vorik curled his gargantuan-sized body around hers, and they prepared to sleep together that way, still in *kor-tar* form so that the icy elements around them had no negative effect.

Nancy grunted, wanting closer contact.

Vorik slid his penis into her from behind, that both of them had the constant contact they craved.

They fell asleep, two Bloodmates bound together in every way possible.

Chapter 7

Nancy awoke the next morning in humanoid form. Vorik's body, still in *kor-tar* form, was curled around her, thwarting the iciness of the landscape from adversely affecting her. Without his skin emitting constant, toasty-warm heat, she guessed she'd be dead in the matter of an hour. She shivered at the thought, then snuggled up closer to him as a matter of self-preservation.

Nancy worried her bottom lip as she realized for the first time that Vorik was still in his gargoyle form. She'd seen him that way last night, but last night she had looked at him through the eyes of a similar predator. This morning, right now, she found herself afraid to get her first good look at him through a human's eyes for when she did she would know precisely what it was she had evolved into.

Her memories of the metabolic changes she'd undergone while cocooning weren't numerous. And those that did exist weren't so much memories as they were impressions. A feeling of rebirth, of rejuvenation, of acquiring heightened senses, and of gaining more acute...everything. Eyes that had once required spectacles or contact lenses to see could now scan terrain a mile or more off in the distance. Ears that she'd once considered to be superiorly adept at hearing would now feel deaf in comparison if she was to listen through them again.

Nancy closed her eyes briefly, drawing in a calming breath of air. She needed to see him, she told herself. She needed to know what it was human eyes would see when they looked at him—and when they looked at her. How could she ever hope to go back to earth if...

Dear God, she thought on a pang of emotion, why was the thought of leaving Vorik, a man she'd known all of a week, so horrible? So empty?

She sighed, for the first time sincerely doubting she'd be able to feel sane without him in her life. Not just in her life, but in her constant presence. The reassuring, steady beat of his heart thumping gently against her back did more to quell her restlessness than she wished it did. Because that quelling, that calming, could only mean one thing: she well and truly would go insane without having him near her.

Nancy's head came up slowly, her round brown eyes finding Vorik's alert crimson red ones. He was awake. Awake and in gargoyle form. Her breath caught. They stared into each other's eyes.

In that instant, as she witnessed the sadness in his gaze, as she heard a low, pained sound rumble gently up from his throat, she knew what Vorik was thinking without needing him to mentally or verbally send the words out to her. He was hurting on the inside, wondering to himself if she'd ever be able to truly love a man who was also a beast.

In a rush of impressions she saw Khan-Gor's past swim before her mind's eye, a past that included the closing off of the silver-ice planet called Khan-Gor to outsiders. A fear of their people, namely what their people were able to do genetically, had caused males from other planets to seek them out in an effort to destroy their race.

In a way, it had worked.

For several millenniums the planet had remained shielded in an invisible cloak of ice until all outsiders had forgotten of their existence and the pack leaders felt it was safe to lower their guard a bit. Even then no Khan-Goris had ventured off planet until the situation had become so grim that the males of their species were left with little choice but to look elsewhere for their Bloodmates, for they weren't likely to find them on Khan-Gor.

Indeed, Nancy saw as she closed her eyes, female-born Khan-Goris were all but non-existent, their numbers sparse. Nature, it seemed, had never intended for Khan-Gori males to mate within their own race, a phenomenon that no doubt kept the gene pools aired out and healthy, and kept females who were transformed into predators breeding dominant, robust sons. To breed within the race could cause madness amongst the offspring, and in one fatal case it had created a monster…

She opened her mind further to Vorik and saw a scene replaying in his memories. The memory was of Vorik's father imparting unto his son the telling of a legend, of how he had been the first Khan-Gori male in three thousand years to venture off planet in search of his Bloodmate, how he had found Jana, Vorik's mother, and how he had brought her home.

But nothing, of course, had been quite that simple.

Nancy's heart clenched when she saw Vorik's first memory, a memory that had occurred just moments after his birth. His mother Jana, who had been on the run from Vorik's father at the time, had been frightened of her *kortar* son upon seeing him flutter out from between her legs. So frightened, in fact, that she had refused to hold him in her arms, or to feed him at her breast, after she had birthed him.

Nancy's bottom lip trembled as the scene continued to play out.

Jana, who had refused to shape-shift into her *kor-tari* form beyond her first emergence from the cocoon, had spent the next few days staring off into space unblinking, a blank expression on her face. Vorik had cried often from within their hiding place, the cries of a newborn baby needing fed. But she had ignored him, hearing nothing, seeing nothing, never acknowledging his existence.

And then one day, thankfully before Vorik had starved to death, his mother had regained her broken mind. Jana had been out of the cave they were hiding in, wandering about aimlessly, when a deadly intruder had snuck in with the intent of killing her tiny son.

His mother, who had been weakened at the time from days of not eating, had sensed the intrusion into the cavern and in a burst of power and speed, had shape-shifted into her gargoyle form and killed the intruder with one swift backhanded slap. Because of the spikes that jut out from a female's arms when in animal form, the kill had been quick and efficient, impaling the enemy and killing him instantaneously.

When it was finally over, and Jana knew that the threat to her son had passed, she had broke down crying, regaining her sanity in the process. *Forgive me, Vorik,* she had sobbed, at last placing the helpless newborn at her breast. *For the love of the goddess, please forgive me, my son...*

Nancy's eyes opened slowly, unspilled tears causing her lashes to glisten as her gaze clashed with her Bloodmate's. Vorik had, of course, forgiven his mother for he loved her fiercely, but his heart had never forgotten the rejection.

Vorik made no movement to force Nancy to stay close to him. He simply laid there and waited for her judgment, his sad crimson eyes flicking over her face. *Can you love me?* she thought she heard him say softly in her mind. *Can you accept me for what I am?*

Nancy's breath caught as she looked at him through the eyes of a humanoid, as she studied his features and found her hand coming up to gently memorize his face with her palm and fingers. His eyes closed briefly at the soothing contact, opening again to watch her expression, to see for himself how she felt.

In that poignant moment, all thoughts of earth, all memories of her former life and friends, dimmed in importance until they had all but faded away. Nancy smiled gently at her Bloodmate, finding nothing lacking, realizing as she did that he was the most powerful and glorious life-form she'd ever been granted the privilege of seeing.

He was carved of sleek silver, his muscles plentiful and fierce. His face, even in *kor-tar* form, was harshly handsome. Though he was bald like any gargoyle would be while in this form, she found the effect made him appear all the more formidable and virile…not to mention terribly sexy.

"Yes," she murmured, her eyes meeting his. She smiled, searching his face. "I can love you."

His breathing hitched as he stared at her, but he spoke not a word. And then, in the blink of an eye, he picked her up in his arms and flew off at top speed, neither descending nor slowing until they reached the cavern she'd incubated in while evolving in the cocoon.

He laid her down gently on a bed of animal hides, then came down on his knees before her, still in *kor-tar* form. Nancy experienced a moment's panic when he splayed her thighs wide before him, then bent his head and licked from her anus to her clit in one wet, rough swipe. She remembered how violently they'd mated as gargoyles the evening prior, so she felt a slight hesitation as it became apparent that he wanted to mount her while she was still in human form.

Their gazes locked. "I shall never hurt you, little one," he said softly. He took a calming breath. "Please do this thing for me, that I might know in my heart you accept me as both man and beast."

Nancy smiled gently, unafraid. She knew he'd never hurt her. She'd only needed the reassurance. "Okay," she whispered back in his language.

His breath rushed out as he lowered his face between her legs and lapped at her pussy with his rough tongue. She gasped immediately, for his tongue in *kor-tar* form was even more abrasive than it was in humanoid form, which sent tremors immediately jolting through her. When she considered the sinfully provocative sight they made, a human woman who was willingly spreading her legs for a gargoyle's wicked sexual ministrations, her nipples hardened into painfully tight peaks.

Nancy glanced down to where his mouth was lapping at her flesh and shivered with arousal. His silver gargoyle face was pressed against her pussy, his crimson eyes watching her as he suckled her clit. He built her to a peak in a matter of moments, the sucks he made to her clit so fast that it looked as though he was munching on her flesh. She groaned, her head falling back against the animal hides, her eyes closing as her nipples jutted up in arousal.

"Vorik."

He suckled on her clit harder, his rough tongue simultaneously flicking the sensitive head in a show of sensual accomplishment no human male could ever master. She bucked up on a groan, then wrapped her legs around his neck and pressed his face in closer to her pussy.

Vorik growled against her clit, vibrating it even as he sucked and flicked at it. Nancy screamed in pleasure, gasping out his name as her entire body convulsed on a loud moan of completion. Blood rushed to her face, heating it. Blood rushed to her nipples, elongating them. Vorik raised his head from her soaked flesh, then curled his rough tongue around one jutting nipple, soothing it while simultaneously further arousing it. She sighed contentedly, her eyes still closed as she stroked his gargoyle head.

And then, oh lord and then, Vorik raised his silver head from her breast, licked her nipple one more time, then settled his huge silver body so he sat on his knees between her legs. He lifted her hips, his fingernails scoring them.

"Oh yes." Nancy's breathing grew choppier, her nipples harder, as she watched the sinful display of a gargoyle—a male many humans would call a demon—mount her pale white body, the body of a human woman.

His crimson eyes met her wide brown ones. His lips parted in a slight snarl, baring his fangs. She licked her lips, recognizing it as a gesture of arousal on his part. She moaned when his fingernails raked her hips again before his large hands reached her thighs and spread them apart.

On a growl he entered her, seating himself fully, his crimson eyes narrowed into slits of desire. Nancy groaned as she watched his silver cock invade her human body, the sight of her wet pussy sucking him into her flesh an erotic one. "Vorik," she breathed out, reaching up and running one finger along his left incisor. He shivered in reaction. "Feed from me," she murmured.

His scarlet eyes widened, not having expected her to accept that part of their mating so soon, so fully.

He growled as his fangs pierced the tender flesh of her neck, his hips rocking back and forth to pound inside of her as he drank of her blood. Nancy came violently, instantly, her moans and groans echoing throughout the cavern as he feasted at her neck, as her body quivered and convulsed from the fierce contractions.

"Vorik."

His gargoyle head raised from her neck, their gazes clashing as he concentrated on mounting her. She saw his teeth grit as he staved off his orgasm, knowing as she did that he wanted a longer mating before he came.

From somewhere deep inside of himself he must have found his control, for Nancy's breath caught as she watched through human eyes while her Bloodmate took her in his beast form. He went wild, primal, his fangs baring fully as he sank his cock into her over and over, again and again.

She screamed from the pleasure, knowing every orgasm erupting from within was as much from watching a gargoyle fuck her as from the fucking itself.

Vorik rotated his hips and slammed into her, his fingernails grazing gently at her hips. His low growl lasted the entire time, throughout every of her orgasms, throughout the entire mating ritual.

When he could stand no more, when he thought he'd go insane if he didn't come, he pounded into her one last time, then on a dominant roar, spurt his hot cum deep inside of her.

Minutes later when the urgency had passed, Nancy found herself once again snuggling up against her Bloodmate to sleep. Only this time it wasn't the body of a female predator seeking the warmth and security of the beast. It was the body of a humanoid woman.

Chapter 8

One week later

Nancy awoke first, standing up after slowly disentangling their bodies. Last night she had played Fay Wray to his King Kong again, wanting him to take her in his *kor-tar* form rather than in his humanoid form, and had thoroughly enjoyed every wicked moment of it. She wasn't certain why really, couldn't explain why it was that she had felt—and still felt—so aroused by something so simple as her Bloodmate mating her while he was shape-shifted, but making love with a gargoyle had a lot to recommend it...

She blew out a resigned breath, smiling to herself. She more than loved Vorik. She was *in* love with him as well.

Hadn't the tiniest part of her, as unrealistic as she'd always known it was, secretly wished Fay Wray would fall as in love with King Kong as the giant ape had with his tiny human captive every time the old black and white movie had been shown on TV? But the real Fay Wray never had, for every time the movie played, she was as desperate to escape King Kong as she'd been the last time. And an hour later, the beloved beast would be dead, having fallen from atop the Empire State Building in his desperation to recapture the tiny woman he loved.

Nancy's eyes closed sadly as the truth hit her. If she ever ran from Vorik, the same fate would befall him. He'd do anything, including give up his life, just to be able to hold her in his arms. The thought of another male anywhere near her would kill him in a fundamental way no human mind could truly grasp. But because of their blood bond, because of the fact her genetics had been altered, she was able to understand.

She *did* understand. And because she did, she knew she would never leave him. Not that she had planned to any way. As frightening as this new world was, Khan-Gor was now her home and Vorik was her mate. As terrified as she was to face what the future held, she realized with gut instinct that the future most definitely did not hold earth.

Besides, she thought with a harrumph, she had fangs now. Fangs and wings. She could turn into a gargoyle. And she had orgasms every time she drank blood. Good grief! As if she could go back home! She'd either be locked up in a mental ward, or studied in some weirdo's lab for the remainder of her days.

Nancy's eyes flicked over to where Vorik slept, his humanoid body relaxed in deep slumber. She smiled. Her gentle giant. He looked so innocent while sleeping, even though she knew that awake he was as fierce as a raptor.

She studied him a moment longer, then glanced away from her mate, her mind fast-forwarding to later on in the day when they would arrive on F'al Vader lands. They had taken their time getting here, wanting to further explore each other's minds and bodies before Vorik took her back to his lair.

Maybe, just maybe, Nancy told herself, joining his pack wouldn't be as frightening as she'd been telling herself it would be. She knew, after all, that Vorik would never hurt her. Nor would he allow another to do so.

He loved her — he was in love with her, and the last week they'd spent together, making love and hunting together, talking about nothing and everything, laughing together—all of it had only further solidified their special bond. And the lovemaking. Oooh the lovemaking...

As her hourly need came upon her, Nancy allowed her form to shimmer and transform into her other, *kor-tari* self. She grinned, her fangs exploding from her gumline as she did so.

She heard her mate awaken from behind her, roused by the scent of her arousal. His lips formed a snarl as he bared his fangs and shape-shifted, growling as he exploded in the air toward her, their bodies clashing.

Nancy hadn't mated Vorik while in *kor-tari* form since the evening she'd emerged from her cocoon. She hissed when his sharp nails dug into her flesh, deciding to immediately remedy that oversight.

To hell with going back to earth. Her eyebrows wriggled.

Naughty Nancy was home at last.

Epilogue

Ten Yessat years later

Nancy F'al Vader, nee Nancy Lombardo, grinned down at the tiny newborn pup feeding at her breast. She'd delivered five litters in ten years time, though her first and last birthings had produced only one son apiece. Thank God.

Nancy still grimaced when she remembered the long, painful ordeal of the fourth birthing two years past. She had delivered five sons in that litter. Five! By the time the runt had made his way into the world, his tiny gargoyle body emerging from between her legs and taking flight, Nancy had begun to feel like a vending machine.

She smiled at the memory, recalling the way her tiny son had flown into her arms the minute he saw her, snuggling against her body and sighing contentedly. The same as another son, her youngest son, was doing now.

"He is perfect," Vorik murmured, his silver eyes finding his Bloodmate's dark ones. He glanced back down at tiny Xorak and gently ran a finger over the small *kor-tar* head. "Just like thy mother."

Nancy snorted at that. "You're just trying to get in my good graces," she teased. "So I don't throw you out of bed again."

He grunted at the recent memory, not having a care for it. "Can I help it if I go off into snoring fits after you've sated me in the bedfurs?" His eyes narrowed, flicking from silver to crimson. "Verily, 'tis a crime and a travesty to deny me thy body, *vorah*." His hand slashed definitively through the air. "I will never allow thus again, whether or not it causes me to snore."

She harrumphed, reveling in the debate. She couldn't help it. The lawyer in her, she supposed. "You gargoyles are all alike," she goaded him. "If ya can't take the lovin, stay out of the oven."

Vorik bent his dark head and nipped her on the shoulder, eliciting a yip. And a shiver. When his face reemerged into her line of vision, his expression was solemn. "Jesting aside, little one, I thank you for yet another beautiful son." He kissed the tip of her nose, then smiled. "I love you, Nancy," he murmured.

He pronounced her name *Nawncy*—always made her smile. She ran her hand gently over his jaw. "I love you too, Vorik."

Later that eve, when all the pups were abed, Vorik joined her in their bedfurs with a wolf-eating grin on his face, a dimple popping out on either cheek. "Shall we play the *yenni* game anon, little one?"

Nancy ran her tongue seductively across her lower lip. She knew how much Vorik loved the *yenni* game. She would pretend to be a starving, voracious alpha *yenni* at market, while her Bloodmate played the role of the horny virgin trader desperate to feed her. Not too far off base from how they'd originally found each other, she thought bemusedly.

She wiggled her eyebrows at him. "I think that old sword is around here somewhere." She snorted. "You remember my sword? The one you mistook for a *yenni* tail ten Yessat years ago?"

Vorik chuckled at the memory. "Aye."

Nancy smiled at her Bloodmate, vastly contented. With him. With their sons. With herself. With life.

She was glad she hadn't taken that job in Alaska. Very glad indeed. Life was beautiful.

Enough said.

About the author:

Jaid Black welcomes mail from readers. You can write to them c/o Ellora's Cave Publishing at P.O. Box 787, Hudson, Ohio 44236-0787.

Also by AUTHOR:

- Death Row
    - The Fugitive
    - The Hunter
    - The Avenger
- God Of Fire
- Politically Incorrect Tales
    - Stalked
- Sins Of The Father
- Taken
- The Hunted
- The Obsession
- The Possession
- Trek Mi Q'an
    - The Empress New Clothes
    - Seized
    - No Mercy
    - Enslaved
    - No Escape
    - No Fear
    - Dementia
    - Guidebook
- Tremors
- Vanished
- Warlord

Why an electronic book?

We live in the Information Age—an exciting time in the history of human civilization in which technology rules supreme and continues to progress in leaps and bounds every minute of every hour of every day. For a multitude of reasons, more and more avid literary fans are opting to purchase e-books instead of paperbacks. The question to those not yet initiated to the world of electronic reading is simply: *why?*

1. *Price.* An electronic title at Ellora's Cave Publishing runs anywhere from 40-75% less than the cover price of the exact same title in paperback format. Why? Cold mathematics. It is less expensive to publish an e-book than it is to publish a paperback, so the savings are passed along to the consumer.
2. *Space.* Running out of room to house your paperback books? That is one worry you will never have with electronic novels. For a low one-time cost, you can purchase a handheld computer designed specifically for e-reading purposes. Many e-readers are larger than the average handheld, giving you plenty of screen room. Better yet, hundreds of titles can be stored within your new library—a single microchip. (Please note that Ellora's Cave does not endorse any specific brands. You can check our website at *www.ellorascave.com* for customer recommendations we make available to new consumers.)

3. *Mobility.* Because your new library now consists of only a microchip, your entire cache of books can be taken with you wherever you go.
4. *Personal preferences are accounted for.* Are the words you are currently reading too small? Too large? Too...**ANNOYING**? Paperback books cannot be modified according to personal preferences, but e-books can.
5. *Innovation.* The *way* you read a book is not the only advancement the Information Age has gifted the literary community with. There is also the factor of *what* you can read. Ellora's Cave Publishing will be introducing a new line of interactive titles that are available in e-book format only.
6. *Instant gratification.* Is it the middle of the night and all the bookstores are closed? Are you tired of waiting days—sometimes weeks—for online and offline bookstores to ship the novels you bought? Ellora's Cave Publishing sells instantaneous downloads 24 hours a day, 7 days a week, 365 days a year. Our e-book delivery system is 100% automated, meaning your order is filled as soon as you pay for it.

Those are a few of the top reasons why electronic novels are displacing paperbacks for many an avid reader. As always, Ellora's Cave Publishing welcomes your questions and comments. We invite you to email us at service@ellorascave.com or write to us directly at: P.O. Box 787, Hudson, Ohio 44236-0787.

Printed in the United States
16623LVS00001B/130-135